D1521552

LEGION
LAKE

by

Robert Kerr

In chapter 22, the poem *Not, How Did He Die, But How Did He Live?*
is attributed to an anonymous author.

Cover artwork by M. Joyce Green

DISCLAIMER

This is a work of fiction. Names, characters, places, and incidents are either products of the author's imagination or are used fictitiously. Any resemblance to actual persons, living or dead, business establishments, events, or locales is entirely coincidental.

Dedication

This book is dedicated to my dear friend, Dave Hutchison, who sadly left us too soon. Taken before he got to know the joys and pains of old age, his passing has left a void in my life that I find myself trying to fill.

A master woodworker and carpenter, Dave started me on my adventures in DIY home improvement shortly after I met him in 1976. He made sure I stayed with it until I was bitten by the bug, and I never recovered. The skills he taught me and the passion he instilled in me have manifested in endless hours working on the houses we have owned since then and inspired my first book, *Completely Restored.*

Dave was known – and is remembered – for his own brand of sage witticisms. My personal favorite was, "Good enough for who it's for," which he was fond of uttering upon completion of any carpentry task. Though it sounded glib, I never knew Dave to quit any project until it met his extremely high standard of perfection.

I hope Dave knew how much I valued his friendship. But, in case he didn't, I am dedicating this work to him. My only hope is that it's *good enough for who it's for.*

Robert Kerr

Chapter 1

Placing the letter back in his shirt, Lester pulled his phone from his pocket and dialed. The call was answered swiftly with "Sheriff's Department. May I help you?"

"Yes, this is Lester Pierce and I have some information about a crime. Yes, I'll hold." And somewhere just off the shore from Lester's dock, a huge walleye swam away contentedly. But then I get ahead of myself. This story actually started...at the Bait Shop.

* * *

The 450 acre body of water, known as Legion Lake, due west of Iowa City, gives its name to a typical Iowa lake community; surrounded by cabins ranging from weekend retreat fishing shacks to year-round homes. Its proximity to Iowa City makes it a favorite place for university-types to live out their own version of Thoreau's idyllic existence (until the weather gets too uncomfortable or their supply of wine runs low). But mainly it is the favorite fishing spot for retired geezers looking to land the big one or at least to find a spot secluded enough that they can lie about it without fear of any witnesses to the contrary. The seclusion, the privacy, the sense that nothing ever happens to separate one peaceful day from the next is what draws the sometimes inhabitants, week after week. And that is usually the case at Legion Lake. Usually.

As for the fishing, what good are lies without a stage for telling them? And that stage is the Legion Lake Bait Shop and Coffee Spot, the community's one and only gathering place for coffee, news and most importantly, gossip. Oh, and lies about the fifteen-pound walleye rumored to live in the lake, known respectfully as Old Wally to the local liars. Lies that help Ruthie, the Bait Shop's proprietor, make a tidy profit in bait and tackle sales every season.

* * *

"Looks like the DNR's out taking water samples again," Lester said as he squinted through the plastic covered window at the brown pickup parked by the shore that had Department of Natural Resources stenciled on the side.

"Why the heck do they even bother with that? Don't they know this lake has always had some contamination? Probably always will?" asked Frank.

"Gives 'em something to do, I reckon," chuckled Lester.

Another answer to Frank's question came from a thin young man with long dark hair seated across the room. "Actually, they're monitoring the levels of Escherichia coli or 'E. coli' as most people know it. This lake, like most Iowa lakes, does normally have E. coli present in it, but one strain, E. coli O157:H7, can be deadly. The DNR monitors the E. coli levels primarily to detect that strain and then will post warnings if it is found."

In an E.F. Hutton moment, all conversation stopped as the occupants of the coffee shop turned and stared at the thin young stranger who had so succinctly summarized the DNR's undertakings. Unaware that he had also painted himself as both a smart-ass and a bore, he grabbed the nearest shovel and kept right on digging. "I know this because I'm majoring in biology at Iowa and am planning on becoming an epidemiologist," he continued.

As the looks on faces turned from stunned to disinterested, the occupants of the Coffee Spot turned back to their own tables and resumed their conversations. "So, how about those Hawks? Reckon they got a chance this year?" Lester asked Frank.

The young man, looking nearly as bewildered as his audience seconds earlier, rose from his chair and deposited his cup into the container by the kitchen window. He was totally unaware that he had simultaneously violated two very important unwritten rules of the Legion Lake Bait Shop and Coffee Spot. First, he inserted university level science into a conversation primarily intended to communicate mutual dislike for a state government agency. And second, he had referred to the U. of Iowa without mentioning the football team in the same sentence. Clueless as to either faux pas, he moved confidently to the cash register. Without another word, he paid Ruthie, the red-headed proprietor, and stepped out the door.

"I don't know...they took quite a hit losing all those seniors. And, as for the new kids, who knows how many of them will be able to stay out of jail?" observed Frank.

"Yeah, they do background checks for everybody else now days; you'd think they'd check out the recruits to see if they're likely to spend the weekends in the slammer, before they sign them up," Lester chuckled.

Nodding in agreement, Frank pulled a coin from his pocket. "You about ready to put that boat in? They got the docks back in at all ramps now."

As the two friends matched quarters and Frank realized he would once again have to pay Lester's tab, he reached for his wallet and slowly rose to his feet. Lester zipped his jacket and put on his gloves, ignoring Frank.

"Well, how about it? You know Old Wally ain't gonna wait forever," Frank said with a grin.

"You been outside? It's still long john weather out there – the ice hasn't been gone a month yet. Wally's not going anywhere." Shaking his head, Lester waited at the door while Frank settled the bill.

"Hey Ruthie, who was that kid that was in here?" asked Frank.

"Some college kid who works for the DNR wildlife people. Name's Sanford. Brock Sanford, I think."

"Another game warden in training?"

"No, he's here to check on the 'environmental impact' of the wind farm they're putting in south of here."

"What's he doing way up here then? Don't those crews come outta Iowa City?" asked Lester.

"He lives here. You gotta get to know your neighbors better, Lester. He's the one shacking up with the young woman in the rental next to your place."

"Huh! So that's who I hear her screaming at? Wondered who she was always chewing on," observed Lester.

"Good for her!" Frank chimed in. "Maybe she can cut him down to size so we can stand having him around."

"I don't think that'll happen," replied Lester, "From what we can hear, she's usually ragging on him about his long hours and wanting him to pay more attention to her."

"Ah, young love," Ruthie mused.

"And, speaking of 'love,' some of those screams we hear coming from their cabin aren't the angry kind. They're the kind Frank ain't heard in years!" Lester said with a grin and one eye on Frank.

Ruthie smiled warmly at Frank and added, "That's only because your hearing's going, right Frank?"

"There's nothing wrong with my hearing," Frank protested. "What's she talking about, Lester?"

"Never mind stud. I'll explain in the truck." With that, Lester pushed Frank through the open door and out into the spring cold. Zipping his jacket, he leaned into the wind and mentally reviewed the day's work that awaited him. The cabin would have to be completely opened up and made ready for the season by evening if he didn't want to hear about it all night from his wife, Shirley. That meant turning the well back on, getting the air out of the pipes, and re-lighting the furnace – all jobs Lester enjoyed a little less each year. "The pontoon will have to wait, Frank, and so will the fish. Only thing we'd catch today would be frozen fish sticks anyway, as cold as that water is. I'll drop you off and then I gotta get started on our cabin." As Lester turned the key in the black F-150, Frank nodded in agreement, and the two men headed off to begin another season at Legion Lake – a season both would remember as long as they lived.

Chapter 2

"Lester! There's no hot water!" Shirley yelled from the bathroom of the gray, weather-beaten cabin.

"You gotta give it time! I just lit the thing five minutes ago," answered Lester as he opened the bathroom door on his less than happy wife of 50-odd years.

"What am I supposed to do in the mean time? I'm freezing!"

Lester stared at his naked wife as she stood soaking wet in the tub, peering from behind the floral shower curtain. The sight of her nude form stirred the kind of thoughts in Lester that used to occur often without such prompting. "Well, you could dry off and let me warm you up a bit," Lester offered with a wry smile. "You know, they say the best way to avoid freezing is to share the body heat of another person."

Wrapping herself in a towel, Shirley warned, "The only thing you need to warm up is that water heater. Now get out!"

Lester retreated, making mental plans to renew his quest later that day. He opened the door to the utility room without turning on the light. In the dark, he could see the reflection of the flame under the water heater against the painted floor. "You should have all the hot water you'll need in thirty minutes," he called to Shirley as he stepped onto the deck to have a look at the lake. Steam was still rising from the water's surface as the sun fought to warm the air. He could barely make out the high dollar cabins across the lake on the north shore, seasonal homes of Legion Lake's affluent residents. *Even with all the work this place takes, we still made a smart decision to buy out here,* Lester thought to himself.

Sporting her favorite pink jogging suit, Shirley opened the sliding door just far enough to extend a hand with a fresh cup of coffee for Lester. "Thanks for checking the water heater. What else needs to be done?"

"Well, besides walking around the place to look for damage from this winter, the only thing I can think of is..." and turning to look at Shirley "taking a *nap,*" he added with a wicked smile. A "nap" being Lester's euphemism for his favorite activity. Shirley's only response came in the form of a grunt and a slight smile. The smile meaning that he was definitely not barking up the wrong tree and the grunt meaning that there would be no "napping" until Shirley was satisfied that Lester had done everything she thought necessary to ready the cabin. Although he rapidly made a mental list of reasons for a different prioritization of the tasks, he kept them to himself and instead reached through the crack in the door for Shirley's hand. "Come on out here and enjoy this view with your coffee," Lester offered. "The work can wait ten minutes."

"I can have the very same view from here and there's heat," she answered, handing him the business end of the dog leash. "Bogie needs to go out and you need the exercise." Lester could tell that at least for that morning, he was going to have to enjoy the view by himself.

He zipped up his jacket and turned his back to the breeze. "Come on Bogie, you heard the woman. Time to do your duty." The perfect quiet of the morning was broken only by the raucous honking of an occasional inbound flock of geese, a sound Lester had gradually learned to appreciate over the years – not so much for its actual melodic qualities but because of what it foretold. When the geese started returning in large numbers, the warm weather was usually not far behind. He sipped at his coffee as the bulldog sniffed the ground for the perfect location to deposit his droppings. Lester led him quickly away from the lawn out onto the grass of the road ditch. "I've had enough exercise fella, how about you?" Bogie's only response was to start the circular dance that signaled that he had either found the perfect location or that he was tired of looking. Lester hung the handle of the leash over the house number sign post on the shoulder of the road. As Bogie finished his business, Lester held the cup in both hands to warm his fingers and watched as the steam rose slowly from the coffee, mixing with the steam from his own breath. He thought perhaps Shirley had made the right decision after all.

Bogie whimpered, signaling that he was not only finished, but more than ready to return to the warmth of the cabin. Lester took the leash and tried to keep up as Bogie scampered across the lawn and up the steps to the deck. Lester unsnapped the lead from the dog's collar and let him back into the cabin. Just then, he became aware of one more sound competing with the geese to disrupt the perfect quiet of the lake. A human sound, every bit as obtrusive as the honking, and foreshadowing something far less pleasant than spring. The muffled voices of two people arguing were quickly rising to a chorus of screams, and they were coming from the neighbors in the rental cabin.

Ordinarily Lester would have leaned toward the source or turned his good ear for better auditory vantage, but he knew from experience that once a woman was that pissed, it was too late to worry about why; it was time to clear out. Just then, the hippie biologist, Sanford, emerged on the run, backpack and all, followed closely by a screaming young woman in a bright yellow Hawkeye jersey. She unleashed one more salvo on poor Sanford, something about never spending any time with her, before realizing their fight had gone public. Nodding at Lester, she forced an apologetic smile and uttered, "Morning," before retreating back into the cabin. In the sudden quiet, Lester was sure he heard the door being locked.

Unchaining his mountain bike from the tree next to the rental, Sanford also acknowledged Lester's presence, but without the smile. Walking the bike past Lester's deck toward the road, he paused and explained, "She thinks I should spend every day off with her! I've got other things to do."

"Go figure," Lester observed with a less than supportive tone.

"I've got to collect data for my research."

Lester nodded in agreement, all the while enjoying the fact that this particular misery didn't require his company.

"If I wanted to spend my days off inside cleaning or running around Hy-Vee buying groceries, I wouldn't have moved to a lake for the summer."

"You don't have to explain…I know…relationships are difficult. Yours has nothing on mine."

"Well, I better get going. I'm sorry you had to hear us." And with that he climbed on the mountain bike and rode off down the blacktop road that led to the open stretch of lake shore known as the South Bank.

Although he had never considered himself a hippie, Lester definitely remembered when he considered himself young, perhaps even virile. And, although he did not yet *like* Brock, he couldn't help smiling as his mind leafed through the pages of the life Mr. Sanford and the young woman he lived with surely had together. At 74, images of Lester's own long-lost youth were hard to come by, but he still enjoyed the view. Turning to go inside, he was still shaking his head and chuckling to himself when he turned and saw Shirley standing in the open doorway, arms crossed, her smile gone and along with it any hope of their "nap."

Chapter 3

Sensing that he had just snatched defeat from the very jaws of victory, Lester abandoned his plan for another cup of coffee on the deck in favor of the immediate commencement of the day's tasks. Without so much as acknowledging the presence of either Shirley or her scowl he exited the deck and rounded the corner to the garage at which point he heard the resounding thud of the patio door being slammed shut. Setting a new personal record, he retrieved the lawn cart and rake from the garage and pressed them into service in less than two minutes. Winters at Legion Lake always leave behind calling cards and the latest one was no exception. Lester could see that the raking alone was surely going to bring back the aches and pains he and the extra-strength aspirin had worked so hard to eliminate all winter.

Lester's cabin and the rental next door were separated by little more space than what was required for the two single driveways and the narrow median of grass between them. Raking that patch placed him within twenty feet of the rental. As Lester took his first break to lean on the rake handle and catch his breath, he could hear the muffled cries of the woman coming from the back porch, broken by short attempts at speech. As he strained to listen, he realized she was talking to someone on her cell – to someone other than Brock. Someone so sympathetic that he suspected it had to be another woman; undoubtedly "Momma." And from the young woman's half of the conversation, Lester could tell Momma was ripping Brock a new one in absentia. *Poor bastard*, Lester thought. *He should get out now while the getting's good!*

Returning to raking the leaves that threatened to kill the grass they smothered, Lester couldn't help thinking about his own mother-in-law, and the fragile truce that had allowed the two of them to co-exist and share holidays without the assistance of counselors or peace officers. Early on, he realized that answering her every salvo with, "You might be right," was an easy enough price to pay for a little peace. And, since her death 15 years ago, the two of them had gotten along quite well. Lester chuckled at his own little joke.

Hitching the lawn cart to the riding mower, he gathered up the piles of leaves and prepared to haul them off to the dumpsite. But, before he made it out of the driveway, Dalton Moore, the Legion Lake DNR ranger, pulled across the driveway blocking his exit. Obviously, this was an unofficial visit or Dalton would have pulled into the driveway.

"What can I do for you, Constable?" Lester asked, cutting the engine.

"Nothing. I just stopped to say hi," explained the ranger. "How have you been?"

"Shirley and I made it through another winter. Yourself?"

"That's good to hear," Dalton answered. "I'm fine. Thanks for asking."

"Could I interest you in some coffee? Shirley just made a fresh pot," Lester offered. He always offered Dalton coffee, even when it was late enough in the day or hot enough that lake etiquette would require something cooler or stronger. "No thanks, I just had some."

"What kept you busy this winter?"

"The usual mostly, ice fishermen, deer carcasses, pushing snow, and jumping dead batteries. That and dealing with the hog confinement Wickham is planning."

"Wickham? He lives at least 50 miles from here. What's the problem?"

"He's got an option on land two miles west of the lake and plans to put in a 5,000 head hog-confinement operation on it," Dalton explained.

"He can't do that! What about the pollution of the lake? And the smell?"

"Well, he's already picked up the paperwork for the permits and as long as he follows the guidelines for the design of the waste containment and all the other requirements, the DNR will have to approve them. DNR biologists take water quality samples weekly during the summer. That might establish a baseline of the water quality if they're collecting the right data, but who knows. As for the odor, well, you might want to invest in some good nose plugs."

Setting the brake on the rider, Lester turned in the seat, his face hardened. "There has to be something we can do, I mean, this will *ruin* the lake!"

"Well, that's really why I stopped. The DNR will hold public meetings as part of the process of approving the permits, but the residents out here are holding a meeting of their own to get some awareness started and form a response to the permit request. It'll be Thursday evening at the Community Building. I thought maybe you and Shirley would want to attend."

"Damn right, we will! And we'll bring everyone else we can get!"

"Well, a committee was formed last month and they are supposed to be getting the word out, but I thought as long as I saw you, I'd tell you myself." Dalton reached for the ignition and then paused. Looking Lester in the eye, he added, "I knew you'd understand the seriousness of this; not everyone out here does. See you Thursday evening." With that he started his truck and drove off.

Lester remained on the rider and processed what he had just learned. *"Wickham? That rich chicken-shit bastard! What's he thinking? He brings that honking big boat out every spring, docks it at the marina and parks its huge tandem-wheeled trailer in the road right where grass grows tall enough to hide it from sight most of the summer. And then, he cruises the lake on it a couple of Sundays a month just to show everybody he's the big dog on the lake. He built that mammoth cabin on the north end over twenty years ago. Doesn't he realize what this will do to everyone's property values, including his? He's probably already got it sold. If he thinks we're gonna stand for this, he's nuts!"*

Lester started the rider and drove off toward the dump site. He knew if he wanted to continue enjoying the retirement he and Shirley had worked so hard for he had to find a way to put a stop to Wickham's plan – even if it took all summer. And, looking at the little red rental cabin next door, he thought he knew where he had to start.

By the time Brock returned to the cabin just before noon, Lester had made three more trips to the dump site and considerable progress toward being back in Shirley's good graces. He had hoped to catch Brock as he returned and bring him up to speed on Wickham's plans, but before he could intercept him, Brock had rolled in on his mountain bike and entered the cabin, leaving his orange backpack hanging on the handlebars. Lester listened intently for the commotion he was sure would follow, but to his surprise, all he heard was muffled, "I'm sorry's" and "Me too's" followed by a long silence. Even Lester knew that it would surely be a while before he would be able to compete for Brock's attention.

Making his final trip to dispose of the yard debris, he mulled over the best way to approach the hippie biologist about his help. He'd have to emphasize the impact on the environment since the blue mountain bike was probably the only property Brock owned. He desperately wanted to get the DNR bureaucrats to listen to common sense, but he knew that would never happen. He hoped the kid would know how to present the right facts to persuade the other property owners to put up enough of a fight to stop Wickham's idiotic plans. And, it would be essential to get all the others at the lake to put their fishing and boating on hold long enough to attend the meeting and understand what was at stake.

Lester knew he'd be able to talk to Brock eventually, but for now he needed to make some calls, a lot of calls.

Chapter 4

It was midafternoon before Brock emerged from the love nest in running shorts and a t-shirt. Looking both satisfied and spent, he sat on the porch rail of the cabin mopping his brow with a towel. Watching from his own deck, Lester wanted to invite him over, but couldn't decide whether to offer him a beer or shower him with Gatorade. Before he could do either, the young woman emerged from the kitchen door in a t-shirt and little else, wrapped her arms around his neck from behind and planted a big wet kiss on his cheek. "You hungry, hon?"

"I'm starved. Do we have any tofu left?"

"I'll see what I can scare up for my man!" she answered with a grin. After giving him another kiss, this time on the lips, she backed away and returned to the cabin.

Lester thought he'd better act quickly before he had to separate them with a fire hose. "Afternoon, Brock. Got a minute?"

"Sure. What's up?"

"There's a meeting at the Community Building Thursday night that I think you'd be interested in, since you're into the lake environment and all that. I'd like you to be my guest; you and..." Motioning in the direction of the woman watching from the deck next door, Lester realized he had no suitable way to refer to her.

"Ashley?"

Lester nodded.

"I'm sorry, I thought you had met Ashley. Ashley Edwards, my roommate."

Lester fought back a smile, thinking that she was a roommate in the same way that Shirley was his houseguest. "Yeah, Ashley then. We'd like you and Ashley to be our guests tomorrow night. Seven o'clock. We'll pick you up."

"What's this meeting about?"

"It's an organizational meeting of residents out here at the lake to form a response to the DNR about a permit to build a hog confinement facility two miles upstream."

"Are you fucking kidding me? Do you have any idea what those things can do to the environment? Hell yes, I'll be there!" Brock rose to his feet and made a beeline toward Lester's deck.

"I thought you might be interested. You probably know way more about these things than most of us out here do. But we're smart enough to know that if it goes through life out here won't ever be the same."

"The impact on the water quality alone would be enough to ruin the lake. And I don't even want to think about the effect on the air. Two miles upstream you say?"

"That's what we're told. So you and Ashley are in?"

"Hell yes! We wouldn't miss it! And I've got a few questions for the DNR myself. I've been collecting some water samples on my own to try to identify the source of the E. coli in this lake."

"Great!" Lester answered extending a hand to seal the arrangement. "We can use all the help we can get. It'll give us a chance to get to know our neighbors. Oh, yeah, I'm Lester. Lester Pierce. And my wife, Shirley, is inside."

"Great to meet you, Lester. Did you say this is an organizational meeting?"

"Yeah."

"Is the ICEP involved?"

"The what?"

"The Iowa Citizens for Environmental Protection. They're absolutely essential to any effective opposition to a CAFO."

"A what?"

"A confined animal feeding operation," Brock explained.

"I really don't know about those things...but I had a feeling you would."

"Well we need to get them involved. What about petitions? Has anyone started a petition or written a letter to the developer? You have to do that first and then request a hearing with the county supervisors to lodge a formal protest, which will be followed by a hearing with the DNR. Has anyone requested a copy of the county's master matrix?"

Lester's brow furrowed as he considered Brock's questions. In an uncharacteristic move, he actually considered his response for a few seconds and then, putting his hand on Brock's shoulder, replied, "Is all that really necessary...how do you know all that?"

"Environmental Activism last semester. Trust me, we'll need to do every bit of it and more if we're going to put a stop to this effectively!"

"Well, this is the first meeting, so you can explain all that to the group Thursday evening. I'm glad you're on our side in this!"

"Brock?" Ashley

yelled from the kitchen.

"You'd better go. Not a good idea to keep 'em waiting. We'll see you tomorrow night."

Satisfied that Brock's interest in the project was sufficiently piqued, Lester returned to his cabin to plan the remainder of his assault on Wickham. Reasoning that anyone who owned property on the lake would at least be concerned about the existence of the hog lot, he located the County Assessor's web page and printed a list of property owners at Legion Lake. As Shirley looked up their phone numbers, Lester called each owner and explained why their attendance at the meeting was essential. Although confronted with the usual list of excuses for sidestepping one's civic duties, by day's end, he and Shirley had successfully extracted promises to attend the meeting from a total of 98 property owners. Shirley was pleased; Lester hoped for more, but needed to move on to Phase II of his plan. And that would require a road trip and calling in a few favors, starting with Brock.

* * *

By Thursday afternoon, the plan was in place. Lester returned from his trip in his pickup pulling onto the blacktop that encircled Legion Lake towing his cargo and slowly circumnavigated the lake in low gear, hazard lights flashing. He waved from the driver's seat while Brock followed suit from the passenger side. Virtually everyone he drove by turned to scope out his vehicle and the contents of the implement it towed.

"I've got to hand it to you Mr. Pierce, this was brilliant!" Brock observed.

"Lester. Call me Lester. Mr. Pierce was my father."

Brock's brow furrowed as he processed the request, nodding eventually in agreement. "Well, anyway, it was a great idea. This should definitely get the point across."

"I think it will help, but most of the people out here view this as their place to escape stress; they aren't used to having to fight for anything *here*. I think it'll take a real jolt to get them actively involved in fighting this."

"Like what?"

"I'm not sure, really. I hope you can paint a picture for them of what the real effect will be, not just on the environment, but on their daily lives."

"But the environment is everyone's life, don't they know that?" Brock questioned.

"Yeah, they all understand that at some level, but what they need to hear tonight is what the immediate effects will be, how a hog farm two miles away will impact them and their ability to enjoy their lake property."

"Don't worry, I get it." Brock assured, brushing his long black hair back with his hand and adjusting his ball cap. "Hey, would you mind letting me out up here by the bridge? I want to take a few more samples. I can walk home from here."

Lester slowed to a stop and Brock opened his door.

"OK, we'll see you tonight about seven?"

"Let's make it ten 'til. And when you paint that picture for them...think Grant Wood, not Jackson Pollock, OK?"

Brock's puzzled look turned to a broad smile as he nodded. "Got it!"

Lester pulled away as the woman across the street saluted him and his cargo by shaking a clenched fist held high in the air.

Chapter 5

"Shirley, remember you're driving!" Lester reminded.

"I'll be out in two minutes!"

"Come on! You'll be the hottest dish there; all the men will be watching you."

Shirley emerged from the bedroom looking her very best. Her silver hair carefully styled just as it had been for more than twenty years. Smiling, she announced, "OK, I'm ready. Let's go."

"Wow! You clean up real nice!" Lester mocked. "I'd ask you out myself, but I'm already spoken for."

Swatting him on the arm, Shirley pulled the keys from her purse and added, "You don't look too bad yourself, you old goat."

By the time they reached Shirley's car, Brock and Ashley were already making their way across the drive toward the red Focus.

"Brock, Ashley. Meet my wife, Shirley Pierce."

"Hey, nice wheels, Mrs. Pierce!" Ashley admired.

"Call me Shirley.

"Too bad it's not electric. Fossil fuels are the number one cause of global warming," Brock observed, unconsciously dampening the moment.

"So are you two a couple or just *friends*?" Shirley asked, handily returning the ball to Brock's end of the court; advantage in. Fortunately, with Ashley up front with Shirley and Brock in the back, neither of them could see the other's expressions.

From the back seat, Lester caught the glint in Shirley's eye briefly as she adjusted the mirror and could tell she was about to serve one up for game point. Realizing the subject was badly in need of changing he asked, "So, Brock...what did you come up with for talking points tonight?"

"Well, I think people need to come away understanding three things; the impact of swine manure on air and water quality, the measures that need to be taken to prevent those impacts, and the likelihood of the eventual failure of those measures."

"You're right. That's just what they need. But remember...Grant Wood."

"That *was* Grant Wood."

Puzzled, Shirley and Ashley looked at each other for clarification that neither could offer.

"I expect this will be pretty informal," Lester added. "Since this is the organizational meeting, we'll be trying to stir up enough concern that people will want to take further action after tonight."

"I called the ICEP and they promised to send someone out to the meeting. I also modified the sample petition from their website and printed twenty copies so we can get started collecting signatures tonight," Brock reported.

"Great work, man!" Lester replied, almost stunned.

"And, after the meeting, you and I and the volunteers on the committee will have to draft a formal letter to the developer as well as a request to the supervisors for a hearing."

Shirley looked at Lester in the mirror, her level of puzzlement matching his look of stunned appreciation.

"Mr. Sanford, I can tell you're going to be a huge asset to us in this!"

"Make that Brock...Mr. Sanford was my old man," Brock answered, giving way to a slight smile.

"Brock's very resourceful," Ashley added.

"Remember, you have to let me out at the old mill," Lester reminded Shirley. "Save me a seat next to Frank and Gloria and I'll meet you there after the thing gets started," he added.

"I know. I know. But it'll just be Gloria; she said Frank's under the weather today," she replied, signaling for the turn onto Mill Road.

"And remember Brock, keep it simple," Lester added as he exited the car.

As he drove to the Community Center on the other side of the lake Lester studied each cabin he passed, reciting in his mind the names of the owners, appreciating perhaps for the first time, the work and money that each family had invested in their property. The neatly trimmed lawns, landscaping, fire pits, picnic tables and decks were proof that they enjoyed the outdoor features of their property most.

Some of the older homes had been in the same families since the lake was created in the early 1900s. No matter what, Wickham had to be stopped!

As he neared the Community Center, Lester's scowl turned to a broad smile. Cars were parked along both sides of the road for two blocks on either side of the entrance indicating a near capacity crowd. And, if that wasn't enough, someone had opened *all* the windows on the lake side of the building. Pulling on to the grass, Lester carefully backed his cargo under the first few windows, locked his truck and quickly entered the building through the kitchen entrance before attracting any additional attention. He stopped briefly to turn on the huge exhaust fan over the grill and then entered the Great Room. Even before he located Shirley and took his seat next to Brock, people in the audience began taking notice of his efforts. After sitting in the sun all day the content of the big green John Deere spreader had reached its prime and was approaching overwhelming. Although Wickham and others got up from their seats at the front table and began shutting windows within minutes, the damage was already done.

"Apparently, Wickham doesn't enjoy the smell of pig shit after all," he whispered as he occupied the chair between Brock and Shirley. Brock smiled broadly in agreement.

Tapping on the microphone, Ranger Dalton Moore asked for the crowd's attention. "Welcome. It's nice to see so many of you here tonight. As I'm sure you all know by now, a request has been submitted for a permit to build and operate a CAFO or confined animal feeding operation...a hog lot...approximately two miles upstream from Legion Lake."

"Booooo!" was the response from several members of the crowd.

Gesturing for quiet, Dalton continued. "I know there is opposition to this, but nothing will be accomplished if we can't hold an orderly meeting. I remind you to refrain from outbursts and to wait your turn to make your comments. A signup sheet is making its way around the room; add your name if you wish to come forward to the microphone and make comments. Everyone will be given an opportunity to speak. But, I think we should start the discussion off by allowing the developer to explain the proposed operation. We'll follow that with questions and input from the floor. And now, Mr. Wickham if you would explain your proposal we'll get things started."

Wickham took the mic and began his explanation. ""I want to thank all of you for coming and giving me this opportunity to explain our operation. I have purchased an option on 80 acres of land located just west of the Donovan farm on 280th St. What I am planning is a small hog operation that would feed hogs to a finished weight and get them ready for market." Smiling his best fake smile he said, "It will provide a few jobs and give me something to do as I ease into semi-retirement."

No one laughed at his attempt at humor.

"Once my permit is approved, we'll close on the land, start building and hope to have the entire structure up and running within six months. It's really not a big deal."

As the crowd's reaction rose to a crescendo, Dalton called for order. "There will be plenty of time for input from the floor!"

"I'd also like to point out that the olfactory treat some joker has provided us this evening is a total misrepresentation of the facts! No modern day hog operation introduces the manure directly into the environment in such a manner. The by-products of our operation will be stored temporarily in an enclosed structure then liquefied and injected directly into the soil of farm land to boost the yields of good old Iowa corn and soy beans. I admire the creativity of the effort, but I had to clear that up. I'm ready to take questions now," Wickham affirmed.

The first speaker rose and approached the mic. "How *small*? How many hogs?"

"No more than 2,500 head at any one time"

Another collective rumble from the crowd greeted that news until Dalton again gestured for order.

"That location is just up the hill from the creek that flows into the north end of Legion Lake. That's bound to ruin the lake!" observed the next person.

"Nothing could be further from the truth. We'll be required to build a manure containment pit complete with liner and safety wall in order to get our permit approved. Trust me, nothing will ever be introduced into the creek or the lake."

"What do you do with the manure when the pit is full?" asked the next speaker.

"As I just said, the liquefied manure will be pumped out at regular intervals and applied to farmland in the vicinity. It will never overflow or leak out so there is absolutely no reason to worry about manure getting into the creek."

"Is that true? How can he say that?" Lester asked Brock.

Rising to his feet, Brock interrupted Wickham. "Mr. Wickham, you paint a rosy picture of your operation. But the truth is that state law and DNR regulations only require the manure containment structure to be 2,500 feet, less than a half mile, from the nearest residence, for an operation of the size you propose."

"Son, you're out of order!" Dalton interrupted. "If you signed up to speak, you'll get your turn."

"Bullshit! Let him speak!" came the response from the floor.

"Don't you mean *pig*shit?" Lester added, getting a huge laugh from the crowd.

"I don't mind at all if the young man speaks," Wickham assured, with his best plastic smile. "Please continue."

"Manure containment structures are no different from any other kind of manmade structure. They last until they fail, until Mother Nature intervenes. Severe storms, earthquakes, etc. can and do cause them to rupture, spilling their toxic contents into the nearest watershed. In one two-year period, there were more than 140 manure spills from CAFO manure management facilities into the waterways of Iowa and surrounding states. In Iowa, the legal limits on manure pit leakage rates allow some structures to leak millions of gallons per year, and studies have shown that more than half of the manure pits in Iowa leak at rates above these limits."

Still smiling, Wickham interrupted, "I don't know where you got those figures, but I doubt very much if that is true!"

"That information and much more like it is available on the websites for the Sierra Club of Iowa, Iowa Citizens for Community Improvement or the Iowa DNR, and yes, those figures are accurate.

Over time, the likelihood of a manure spill into the waters of Legion Lake is quite high."

Brock's response was truncated at this point by applause and hoots of approval from the floor. "But a more immediate concern is the effect your proposed CAFO will have on air quality, since there is no effective way to contain the pollutants and toxins they will release into the air. Air quality and even the very quality of life as we know it here at the lake will suffer drastically if you build a CAFO so close by. Several studies have shown that the odors from hog CAFOs are not just obnoxious and unpleasant. They're actually hazardous to one's health, increasing the incidence of lung diseases, stress-related disorders, gastro-intestinal conditions and they can even impact the functioning of the brain and other organs," Brock continued. "And the economic impact of CAFOs is even more directly traceable. Some Iowa counties have reported an increase of over $6,000 per mile in maintenance costs of the roads used by CAFO support vehicles. CAFOs are eligible for large tax-breaks which reduce the revenues local governments have available for road maintenance. But by far the most serious economic impact is seen in the average 40 percent decline in property values in areas close enough to CAFOs to notice the odor they release."

The uproar this particular information caused was too big for even Dalton to quell. Wickham was noticeably affected by the catcalls and threats from the crowd; he actually backed away from his table and looked to Dalton to intervene. Only when Lester stood, issued an ear-splitting whistle and then asked that Brock be allowed to continue, did relative quiet return to the room.

"Thank you. What I have described so far is admittedly the worst case scenario. But even under the best of circumstances, the impact on the lake and other water resources in the area will be extremely negative. Nutrients in manure, such as nitrogen and phosphorus, will cause depleted oxygen levels in the lake as well as increases in the frequency and duration of algae blooms. Even if everything you will be required to do works as it should, the quality of life for lake residents – both human and otherwise – will be degraded forever!" Turning to the audience, Brock pleaded, "But mostly, you the property owners of Legion Lake, can expect the value of your property to drop precipitously at the same time that your real estate taxes rise sharply to pay for the increased road maintenance. I invite all of you to join me in an effort to block this permit request and prevent permanent damage to Legion Lake and the surrounding environment!"

The same audience that moments earlier had been a virtual sea of blue hair and bald heads, erupted into a tsunami of shouting, applauding, threatening and name calling all of which was aimed at Wickham. Dalton's best efforts to restore order faltered for more than two full minutes until finally, he pulled an air horn from his jacket pocket and let forth one long blast. "Let me remind you one more time that this will be a *peaceful* assembly! No one will accomplish anything otherwise!" With his right hand on the holster of his side arm, his eyes swept the front row as he asked slowly, "Do I make myself clear?"

Just as a dog that has been chastised for barking will reduce it to a low growl, so did the crowd retreat to grumbles and whispers, but Dalton, being no fool, settled. Turning to the head table he asked, "Mr. Wickham, would you like to respond to Mr. Sanford?"

Now Wickham, smiling even more broadly than before, stood and addressed the crowd. "Thank you, Mr. Sanford, is it? I'd love to discuss the finer points of those charges with you, but maybe at a later time. Maybe we could meet over coffee sometime," he said, glaring at Brock. Smiling again and turning back to the audience, "Ladies and gentlemen, I am dead serious when I say the very last thing I want to do is to cause any harm to Legion Lake or to the property values here. As you all know, my wife and I have owned a place here for more than 20 years and have made a sizeable investment in improvements to it over those years. If I thought this agricultural enterprise would in any way cause harm to the environment of the lake or lower property values, I wouldn't pursue it any further. I am absolutely convinced that the effects will be nothing but positive. In fact, I am so certain of this that I will stand here tonight and make the following offer to all of you, in fact to *any* property owner here at the lake."

Even the whispers of suspicion now fell quiet; he had their attention.

"As long as we can keep this permit process friendly and peaceful like, I'm willing to do the following: If *anyone* here at the lake feels their property value is threatened by my proposal, I will buy that property *outright*! I am that certain of the effect it will have; I am that concerned about our lake."

Again his words produced an uproar, but this time it was apparent that while some of the audience members were discussing the meaning of his offer with their nearest neighbor, others simply sat quietly mulling it over in their mind. From that moment on, the tone of the meeting changed.

Reaching for Brock's hand Shirley gushed, "Brock you made the case wonderfully! Don't you agree Lester?"

"Absolutely. It was pure Grant Wood..." Lester replied half-heartedly, his mind much more on Wickham's words than Brock's. In spite of damage done by Brock's summation of the CAFO's effects, Lester feared that Wickham had clearly scored a victory of his own.

As the meeting wound down and audience members milled around the room comparing viewpoints with neighbors, Brock stood again and whistled loudly for their attention. He announced that he had a petition opposing the development and asked people to sign it on their way out. Lester wondered how many would. Clearly, those angered by what they had heard would sign; but another faction seemed satisfied with Wickham's assurances and others, fewer in number perhaps, had a dazed look in their eyes. A look Lester had seen before in eyes that eventually filled with dollar signs.

No doubt Brock had convinced many in attendance to oppose the development, but Wickham had done something even more powerful. Lester knew from his days in the military that a force divided is a force defeated; Wickham had definitely divided the audience and now the battle was on. A battle far more involved than Lester had originally assumed.

Chapter 6

"Lester, are you up yet?" Frank asked as he knocked on the patio door.

"I've been up for hours! I'm back here," came the answer from behind the cabin. "It's 9:15; you been sleeping in?"

Frank trudged around to the back of the cabin and found Lester pulling the tarp off the pontoon. "Yeah, I didn't sleep much last night. I got this cold; kept coughing my head off. And Gloria told me about how the meeting went and I kept thinking about that. She said you wanted to see me. About the meeting?"

"No, I thought since you've been in such a toot to get out on the water, maybe we could put her in today. I'm sure the water has warmed a little with all this sun."

"Hey, that sounds great. I'll do what I can, but this cold has really got me down. Maybe we need another guy to help us."

"Oh, you'll do fine. I can do the heavy work and you can back her off the trailer and drive her over to my dock."

"Alright. So, how'd you think the meeting went?"

"Not great. Brock did a fantastic job, and I thought he had Wickham backed into a corner, but the son of a bitch managed to win over about a third of the crowd by offering to buy anybody out who's worried about property values."

"Think anybody will sell?" Frank asked as he helped Lester spread the tarp on the ground and roll it up.

"Sure. Anybody who was already looking to sell would be a fool not to take him up on his offer."

"Did he say anything about how much he would pay?"

Lester stopped rolling the tarp and looked straight at Frank. "Why? Are you thinking about selling?"

"No! I just wondered how good a deal he's gonna make people. It's one thing to say he'll buy 'em out, but how much he's willing to pay... That's maybe a whole different thing, that's all."

"Well he is a businessman. I don't imagine he's planning on paying any more than what he thinks he can get when he resells later. I hope when people find out what he's offering they change their minds again and decide to join in the fight against the CAFO."

Frank bent down, lifted the heavy roll of tarp part way up to his shoulder and then dropped it to the ground again.

"What's the matter, did that tarp get heavier this winter?" Lester chided.

A very pale Frank only held his hand up to Lester and shook his head without answering. He struggled to catch his breath and Lester thought he detected wheezing.

"Here, you sit down on the trailer tongue and I'll put the tarp away." Returning from the garage, he noticed that the color had returned to Frank's face, but he was still sitting. "Maybe you better rest this afternoon. I can always get somebody down at the ramp to help me with the boat."

"No I want to help, I'll just take it easy. You want to go after lunch?"

"If you're up to it?"

"Don't worry about me, I'll be there," Frank answered as he rose and made his way slowly to his brown, one-eyed Tacoma. "Pick me up as you go by."

Lester waved in agreement as Frank turned the engine over and drove off. Lester returned to the garage and disconnected the boat battery from the charger. As he lugged the heavy, deep-cycle battery around the corner to the pontoon his mind was still on Wickham's plan to build the hog lot. *What the hell's he thinking?* He asked himself. Lifting the battery onto the back platform, he wondered how anyone could think that putting 2,500 head of pigs upwind would be okay for the lake. As he slid the massive battery into place, he tried to move his fingers out of harm's way, but managed to smash his thumb as he let go. "Son of a bitch!" He would have recited even more of the battery's pedigree, had he not heard the screen door on the rental cabin slam shut. Brock scurried off the deck like a man on a mission and headed for the tree where his mountain bike was secured by a cable lock. As their eyes met, Brock put the closed loop of the bike lock cable over his head and one arm and started pushing his bike toward Lester.

"Morning, Lester."

"Back at ya! Everything all right?"

"Yeah...I guess."

"You don't sound so sure?"

"It's Ashley. I guess I just don't understand her." Brock answered, confirming Lester's suspicions. "I mean, she's always on my ass about not spending enough time with her, and, well, it's not as if I'm not attracted to her, as I'm sure you've noticed."

Lester gave his best academy nominated performance to look and sound as if he had no clue about his neighbor's love life. "No...can't say as I have. But, go on."

"Well, that's just it, when I do stay around the house, she acts as if I have the plague or something."

"I don't follow," Lester lied.

"I mean we used to, you know, do it several times a week when I first moved in, but recently... Can I ask you something personal, Lester?"

"Sure, I guess," Lester replied cautiously, not sure if he liked where the conversation was going.

"How often did you and Mrs. Pierce, you know, 'do it', when you first got together?"

Taking full advantage of a sudden coughing jag to buy time, Lester sensed he had stumbled onto a golden opportunity for fun at the young man's expense. "Excuse me...Well, let's see, I think we got it on about three or four times a week at first, like you say, but as we got to know each other and felt, you know, more comfortable, it increased over time. Now we do it at least once a day, sometimes twice," he lied with a straight face. "We even keep track on the calendar."

The look on Brock's face nearly caused Lester to lose it, but he turned just in time toward the open window on the back of the cabin saying, "That reminds me," and yelling to Shirley he asked, "Hey, honey, did you mark the calendar this morning?"

"No, you're supposed to do it as soon as we finish, remember?"

"Well, be a dear and mark it for me. I'm sorry, I forgot."

Turning to Brock as if nothing had happened, he asked, "So, where you headed now?"

Looking every bit as if he was on the verge of crying, Brock answered, "I've gotta collect some more samples while the water is still calm. It's not much fun working out there in a kayak when there're white caps."

"No I suppose not. Say, that's a pretty healthy looking bike lock; you know something about a crime wave out here that I don't?"

"My bike's a Superfly 8 worth over $1,500; I never leave it unsecured!"

Lester threw his pliers down on the pontoon deck and turned to look first at Brock and then at the bike. "Say what? How much?"

"I paid just over $1,700 with tax. It's part of the Gary Fischer Collection, made of Alpha Platinum Aluminum and has hydraulic disc brakes."

"That's more than I paid for my first..." Lester re-considered finishing the thought as he knew it would tell Brock more about *him* and *his* values than he was comfortable with. He came around from the back of the pontoon to have a close-up look. "I'd be afraid to ride a bike that I had put that much into. Is that cable enough security?"

"It would take anyone quite a while to cut it and besides, I registered the serial number with Trek and engraved my name in three places on the frame where nobody's likely to notice."

"I see. So you feel it rides that much better than the ordinary bike?"

"Hell yes! I'd let you take it for a spin, but I need to get going before the wind comes up."

"Well don't let me keep you," Lester offered still shaking his head. "But, say, where are you planning to be around noon?"

"I don't know, what do you need?"

"Frank and I are gonna put this tub in about then; we could use an extra hand."

"Sure, just call my cell."

Checking his pocket for a pen, Lester admitted, "I don't have your number."

"Give me your cell. I'll put it in for you."

Relieved, Lester surrendered his phone. "You really did a nice job last night. I think most people came away much more well-informed about the reasons to oppose the CAFO."

"It's the right thing to do, not just for people's property values, but for the lake and the environment. And it's not the only threat. I keep finding very high levels of E. coli O157:H7 in my samples. The grid pattern I've used points to one particular part of the far shore. I've just about pinpointed the source; it has to be coming from somebody's leaking septic tank."

"Really. One of those rich SOBs over there is poisoning our lake?"

"Looks that way. I'll know more in a few days," Brock assured him as he swung one leg over his bike and prepared to ride off. "Anyway, call me when you're ready to launch your boat."

"I will. But before you go, what about the committee you mentioned? Did anybody volunteer?"

"I took down a few names of guys who seemed interested. And, I drafted a letter last night after I got home."

"Good. What about that group you mentioned...the IPC? What happened to them?"

"You mean the ICEP? The guy called me after the meeting and apologized. He got lost, but I emailed him directions so he could make the next meeting...whenever we hold it."

"I'll call you after lunch. Good luck finding the leaky tank!"

Brock turned and rode off down the street with a level of energy Lester couldn't imagine trying to muster. Within seconds, the blue mountain bike disappeared around the bend into the shadows of the cottonwood trees. All Lester could make out was the bright orange knapsack on Brock's back and then that too was taken from Lester's view by the growing distance. He was still smiling at the thought of Brock believing that he and Shirley "did it" even once a day, but his smile was short lived as he recalled the real reason for the marks on the calendar.

Wiping his hands on a rag, he entered the back door of the cabin and reached into the cupboard over the washing machine. Grabbing the bottle of ear drops, he called "Here, Bogie. Come here, fella." Once he had instilled two drops in each of Bogie's ears, the smile returned once again, not just because of his joke on Brock, but also because he had involved Shirley in it so cleverly without her knowledge.

It was well past two o'clock when he called Brock and pulled out of his driveway towing the faded blue pontoon. When he reached Frank's place a quarter mile down the road, he pulled onto the shoulder and honked. Gloria emerged from the back door of the weathered gray cabin, her silver hair held in check by the hood of her signature Hawkeye jacket. Lester couldn't help noticing the large camera hanging from her neck on the bright gold and black strap. She motioned for Lester to roll his window down. Leaning into the passenger side of the cab, Gloria explained, "Frank's coming. He's just waking up from a nap. He'll be out as soon as he gets his shoes and jacket on."

"Is he feeling any better?"

"I don't know...you know how he is. He's still got the cough. If he's not better by tomorrow, I'm gonna run his butt to the doctor in town for some medicine. You old guys need to take care of yourselves, you know," Gloria reminded Lester with a smile. They both knew her birthday cake had just as many candles as either Lester's or Frank's.

"OK, well, tell Frank to shake a leg. If anything bigger than a Volkswagen comes by I'm blocking the road and I'll have to go on without him. What's with the camera? You joining the paparazzi?"

"No, it's what I decided to spend my uncle's inheritance on. Always wanted a nice one and this one's top of the line. Now I just have to learn to run it," she explained with a grin. "It's very complicated. I had to have Frank's help to set it up, but I'm learning."

Just then, Frank emerged from the back door, buttoning his coat as he trudged to the truck. "I thought you were coming over at noon? I held off on my nap as long as I could," he complained to Lester as he pulled the door shut and yawned.

"Yeah, I can see that. Are you sure you're up to this?"

"Who, me? Sure! It's just a cold's got a hold of me, that's all. You back her in and I'll drive her over to the dock like we planned."

Checking his mirror as he eased the rig back onto the road, he saw Gloria snapping a picture. "Well you don't have to, you know. Brock's coming along to help. He could drive it."

"Brock? What'd you go and invite that dipstick along for?"

"Well, for starters, you weren't the picture of health this morning. I didn't know if you were gonna show. And besides, I'm starting to like the kid. He's doing a great job of helping to put Wickham in his place, and he's looking out for the lake in other ways too. He told me this morning he's just about found the source of that E. coli that's in the lake."

"Well, he's OK, I guess. He just rubs me the wrong way, that's all."

"He's a typical over-educated college kid. Once you get him off the subjects he's been studying at the university he doesn't know his ass from a hole in the ground. But the way I see it, he needs us."

"How you figure that?"

"Well, he needs us to *round out* his education. You know, how to fish, drink beer and get along with women."

Frank turned and looked at Lester. ""Huh?" As the corners of Lester's mouth slowly turned upward, Frank began to understand. "Oh, you mean we need to *initiate* him. Yeah, that could be kinda fun!"

"It already has been!"

As Lester pulled the rig into position for backing down the ramp, Brock rode up and secured his bike to the end of the dock's hand railing with the cable. Frank stepped out of the truck to guide Lester as he approached the dock, but immediately began a one-man recital of coughing and hacking. Stepping in on the driver's side and motioning to Lester, Brock said, "That's it, come on back..."

"Hold it!" Frank shouted and Lester complied. Frank tried twice to get his footing on the trailer tongue.

"Here," Brock offered, "I can get up there."

"I'm fine," growled Frank, "just give me your hand."

Once Frank was on board, Lester continued backing with Brock's guidance. As the trailer wheels reached the crest of the ramp and the stern of the pontoon hung over the water's edge, Brock yelled, "Hold it! Don't we need to raise the motor up?"

Frank tugged on the 40hp Evinrude, without success. "Damn it!" He reached over the back railing to the release and pulled, but his effort again frustrated, he shouted, "Goddamn it, Lester! When are you ever gonna fix this damned release? Give me something to pry it with!"

Lester set the brake and stepped out of the cab. "I meant to. I just forgot about it again." Digging around behind the passenger seat in the area Lester called his "tools," he emerged with a rusty jack handle. He handed it to Brock, who in turn relayed it over the side rail to Frank.

Frank leaned far over the back rail and pried the release open and stood back up to pull on the motor. As he did, the release popped back into the locked position. "Son of a bitch! If this doesn't come loose soon, I'm gonna be one pissed-off Norwegian!"

"You lose my jack handle in the lake and I'm gonna be one pissed-off Irishman!"

"Frank, give me the handle and get ready to pull on the motor," Brock directed. "I'll work the release." With that, he worked his way around to the stern of the boat into knee deep water. "OK, pull."

Once the motor was up, Brock returned the handle to Frank and waded back toward the dock. Frank gave it a throw onto the safety of the dock, but it bounced on past the end and glanced off of Brock's mountain bike, leaving a nice dent in the frame just ahead of the chain rings. Certain that Brock would not appreciate Frank's modification to his precious bike and just as certain that neither he nor Frank had seen what had just happened, Lester took the easy way out and retrieved the jack handle without a word. He released the winch strap and backed the trailer the rest of the way down the ramp until the pontoon floated clear.

Frank dropped the motor down into operating position and turned the key. The motor started hesitantly but smoothed out after a few seconds as it began to warm up. Zipping his jacket all the way up to his neck, Frank waved the all clear to Lester who pulled the trailer up the ramp freeing the pontoon for another season of tormenting the crappies and walleye. "Tell him to come get me at his dock. I ain't in the mood for no hike!" With that he put the motor in reverse and backed away from the dock in a wide arc. Once he was well clear of the dock area he moved the shifter forward to full speed. A minute later Frank was well on his way back across the lake to Lester's dock.

"Come on, put your bike in the back, and I'll take you home so you can change into something dry."

"That's OK, I'll be dried out by the time I ride back home. You need to go get Frank."

"All right then. Meet us at the Coffee Spot and I'll buy you a coffee and one of Ruthie's cinnamon rolls for your help."

"That sounds good. I haven't had lunch yet."

By the time Lester parked the trailer, picked up Frank and drove back to Ruthie's, Brock's bike was already securely fastened to the tree out front. Lester took it as a good sign that he wasn't outside with the bike cussing up a storm about the dent. "Coffee and rolls are on me this afternoon. I owe you," Lester offered. Still hacking, Frank nodded his head in agreement.

During the summer, an afternoon crowd at Ruthie's will seldom be large enough for a game of gin rummy, but in the early spring when it's too cold to be out on the lake, it's often a full house. Once inside, Lester wondered if they could even find a place to sit, let alone expect anything to eat. "Hey Lester, nice to see you and Frank again," Ruthie smiled.

"There's three of us today. Brock's with us."

"I see that," Ruthie explained, pointing with a head jerk toward the large sign over her door which read, "Those who pass through this door bring joy, some when they enter and others when they leave!"

Smiling back, Lester asked, "Any chance you could open up seating for three and bring us coffees and cinnamon rolls?"

"Without a reservation, I'm afraid, all I can offer you is the 'Party Room'," Ruthie replied. "It's the maître d's day off. You'll have to clear the table and find seats yourself."

"Ah, a table by the window. That will do nicely, madam." Lester and Frank led Brock to Ruthie's storeroom where they found an old kitchen table piled high with cases of pop and jugs of cooking oil. Frank began removing the items from the table as Lester dragged a 50-pound sack of potatoes over to one end of the table and opened a two-step stepladder for the other end. Frank reached in the broom closet and retrieved a folding chair for Brock. The two older men took their places as Brock began to realize that this wasn't their first culinary experience in the 'Party Room.'

Ruthie entered the store room from the kitchen carrying a tray with three coffees, one cinnamon roll and three jelly donuts. ""Sorry boys, but I'm down to the last cinnamon roll. Who gets it?"

"I'll take it!" Frank insisted.

"No, I promised one to Brock" Lester corrected, reaching for the paper plate that held the golden evidence of Ruthie's baking talents.

"Really that's OK, I don't care," Brock offered.

"Not yet you don't, but that'll change once you've bitten into it. Frank, you can have the extra jelly donut."

"That's why I brought it. The extra one is on me," Ruthie explained. And, even though Lester had already offered to pick up the tab, the thought of free pastry more than appeased Frank for the moment. Ruthie placed the ticket strategically midway between Frank and Lester and returned to the kitchen to resume living the dream – selling live bait and pastries to codgers could be so rewarding.

"So, Ashley was OK with you spending enough time away to help us with the boat?"

"Well, yeah, I guess so. She said it was fine," Brock answered, aiming his fork at the caramel-draped roll. Frank and Lester made eye contact, briefly smiling, and bit into their own samples of Ruthie's wares.

"Well, she's in for one more season," Frank observed. "But if you don't get that release fixed, this is the last time I'm helping."

"Next fall, as soon as she's out of the water."

"It's a pain in the neck standing on my head over the rail trying to get it to release."

"Kind of like working with a ticked-off Norwegian?" Lester answered.

"About that," Brock interrupted, "you're not really one you know."

"Well, not now. I'm over it now. But next time, if it ain't fixed next year..."

"No," Brock paused long enough to take a bite of cinnamon roll. "I mean you're not really Norwegian. Boy these rolls are the *bomb*."

"What the hell do you mean?"

"They're really good! I see what you mean, Lester."

"What do you mean, I'm not *Norwegian?* I was *born* Norwegian!"

"Well, look at your pigmentation, Frank."

"My what?" Frank demanded.

"Your skin tone. You have olive skin and I'm guessing your hair used to be black?"

"Yeah, so what? My whole family looks like me," Frank assured, "even my ancestors who settled in Minnesota 200 years ago. I've got pictures for God's sake!"

"They settled in Minnesota after they emigrated from Oslo, right?"

"Yes, dammit! Oslo, *Norway!*"

"Where'd you get all this crap? Frank's about the most Norwegian guy I know. He eats Lutefisk for breakfast for cripes sake!" Lester attested.

Glaring at Brock, Frank took a big swig of coffee, burning his lip in the process.

A very pregnant pause overcame the conversation as all three men pondered what had already been voiced.

"All I'm saying is with your darker skin tone and black hair, although your ancestors came over from Norway, before that they undoubtedly were Semites from the Mediterranean, probably Portugal or Spain."

"So?"

By this time even Brock was aware that his welcome was about worn out. He folded the paper plate around the remainder of his roll and took one last sip of coffee. "I didn't mean to offend you, Frank. I was just stating a fact." Another long lull in the conversation followed. Finally, standing, Brock offered, "You can check it out. Google it." Pushing his folding chair back under the table Brock continued to apologize. "I gotta get home. Ashley's probably wondering where I am. Look Frank, it's no big deal. Lots of Norwegian-Americans had ancestors who worshiped in synagogues in the old country. I guess I thought you already knew. Anyway, I'll see you guys later. Thanks for the coffee and roll, Lester." With that, he left the party room and the

Bait Shop clueless as to the amount of joy his particular departure brought.

"What the hell's he trying to say, Lester?"

Lester looked at his Norwegian friend of more than 30 years and took a last sip of coffee. "I think what he's trying to say, Frank, is that even though you prefer fish for breakfast and you're usually the last one to catch on to a joke, you're actually...a Jew."

Frank's brow furrowed deeply as he processed what Lester and Brock had said.

"But right now, I don't think that's the most important thing Brock told us," Lester teased.

"What'd ya mean?"

"Well, remember he said Ashley said it was 'fine' that he spent this afternoon helping us with the boat?"

For the first time since Brock left the Coffee Spot, the frown left Frank's face and was replaced by a broad smile. "Yeah...he's screwed!"

"Soooo screwed!" Lester affirmed.

The two men continued to laugh at Brock's expense as they enjoyed the rest of their coffee and pastries, but deep down, Frank continued to dwell on Brock's news about his lineage. It was news that would forever change Frank Mariboe.

Chapter 7

Shirley Pierce stepped off the deck into the morning twilight with every intention of resuming her routine of a daily walk around the shore to the boat ramp and back, a distance of more than two miles. The morning air was cool, but not cold – perfect weather for sporting her new pink warm-up suit. As she neared the Anderson's cabin and detected the scent of crabapple blossoms on the slight breeze, she couldn't help feeling a bit superior to anyone who didn't have a place on a lake. She daydreamed of afternoons reading on the deck in the shade of their maples and evening cookouts with Frank and Gloria and the gang. But her little birdwalk was cut short when she became startled by a dark form standing next to one of the trees. She stood still in the road searching for some sign of familiarity in the image silhouetted against the eastern horizon. She had just cautiously resumed her advance when a brilliant flash blinded her momentarily.

"Whoa!!" she gasped.

"Shirley?"

"Gloria? Is that you?"

"Good morning. What are you doing out here so early?"

"I was about to ask you the same thing. You about scared the crap out of me," Shirley said a little breathlessly.

"Sorry. I came out to photograph the sunrise. It was so cloudy last night I thought maybe it would be pretty, but it looks like it cleared up during the night."

"I don't think that flash is going to help."

"I know...it's automatic. I forget to turn it off. I still have a lot to learn about this thing. Frank says I cut off more heads than a French executioner."

"How's he doing?"

"He seems to feel better. I think his cough is improving."

"That's good, but I meant how's he taking the news? You know, about what Brock said yesterday?"

"Oh that. I'd have to say he took it hard."

"You don't mean he believes it?"

"Oh yes he does...now!"

"That's silly, if he's not Norwegian, I don't know who is!"

"Well you know Frank. He's been on the computer reading up on the Jews of Norway. And one of those genealogy sites. Turns out, everything the kid told him checks out. He's not happy about it, but I'm sure he *believes* it, now."

"Well...he'll get over it. It would be a shock to anybody to find out that your ancestors weren't who you thought they were. I suppose it would hit you about like learning you were adopted," Shirley offered.

"That's just what Frank says! I keep telling him he's still the same person, but I can tell it's changed him."

"You'd think Brock would have realized that. Sometimes, I wonder what's wrong with that boy!"

"No kidding! He and that woman."

"Ashley? Yeah, she and Brock make a real pair. We can't tell if she's in love or just...in heat!"

"Yeah, I know what ya mean."

"I'd better keep going, my old goat expects breakfast for some reason." Putting her hand on Gloria's shoulder, she added, "Make *your* old goat take care of himself and get over that cold."

"Thanks, I will."

As Shirley resumed her walk, the horizon ahead of her was beginning to take on an orange glow. She chuckled to herself about Frank and the thought of him being anything other than Norwegian. How he so enjoyed sharing stories of his boyhood on the Minnesota farm and growing up outside Spring Grove, which he claimed was the first town settled by Norwegians. How his endless supply of Ole and Lena jokes was only exceeded by his supply of smoked salmon. And, eventually, she caught herself reciting his favorite ditty, "*O Lutefisk, how fragrant your aroma. O Lutefisk, you put me in a coma. You smell so strong, you look like glue, you taste yust like an overshoe. But Lutefisk, come Saturday, I tink I'll eat you anyway.*" No, the bard was right – a rose by any other name... Shirley simply could not imagine Frank any other way but Norwegian, nor could she imagine summers at the lake without him and Gloria. And, with an entire summer ahead, her thoughts returned to reading and cookouts as she once again found her stride.

She had enjoyed her visit with Gloria, but her daily walk was *her* time, and she was going to enjoy what was left of it. Nothing else was going to interrupt her, not even the sound of the car approaching from behind. She moved over to the oncoming shoulder to let it pass. The driver behind the wheel of the massive Escalade roared on past her without so much as slowing down or a honk or a wave. It was the only Escalade she had ever seen at the lake, the silver one owned by Wickham.

She cussed him under her breath as he continued down the road, in part for almost running her over, but mainly just for being Wickham. But no more than 500 feet down the road the brake lights flared bright red as the Escalade slowed to a stop and the unmistakable bright beam of a spotlight shot out of the passenger window onto the cabins on the shore of the lake. *What in the heck...?* she wondered. The Escalade moved again, but stopped only a few feet further down the road. Shirley picked up her pace, hoping to satisfy the curiosity building within her. Again the spotlight cut through the pre-dawn darkness onto the property on the lakeside of the road. *What is he doing, looking for a lost dog?* she asked herself, mentally rooting for the dog to escape detection. The brake lights dimmed a third time, and the Escalade again moved forward. But this time it continued on down the road until the tail lights disappeared around the curve.

Suddenly, the aroma of crabapple blossoms had been replaced by the smell of exhaust fumes and the odor of *pigs*! And although Shirley knew the latter came from her own imagination, it stayed with her long enough to put an end to the enjoyment of her pleasant walk. She stopped and turned back toward the cabin she had shared for more than 30 summers with her husband and abandoned all hope of enjoying her walk; from that point on, it would just be exercise anyway.

Chapter 8

Wickham put the silver Escalade into park in the driveway of the two-story log home. The carriage house style porch light next to the garage door was the sole source of illumination competing with the oncoming daybreak. Miriam was still not up. The less she knew, the better. He remained behind the wheel and commanded Bluetooth to dial for him – a series of rings preceded a half-awake response.

"It's Wick."

Wickham waited as the man on the other end fumbled with his phone and then questioned the hour of the unwelcome wakeup call.

"I'm sorry, did I *wake* you? I thought it was time to talk!" He turned on the map light and opened a manila folder. "I just looked at 4957 and 4959. I thought you said they sat on *double* lots?" He paused as the man on the other end attempted an explanation. "Yes, Hansens and Ulrichsons." He pulled a Cross pen from his jacket pocket. "I don't give a damn *how* you pronounce it! They look too small!" Flipping through the pages in the folder, he separated two from the rest. "Not according to the assessor's measurements." Raising his bifocals to the top of his bald head, he rotated the pages. His beady brown eyes squinted at the data before him. "I don't care what they told you, if I'm buying property, you've got to get me more accurate info than this!"

As the sound of an approaching car made it obvious that he was about to have company, Wickham doused the map light and took his foot off the brake. The car moved on past his drive without slowing. After it was safely down the road, he again turned on the map light. "I don't care what you tell them, just get it. Have that inspector you're so tight with pay them another visit." Nodding his head pointlessly he affirmed, "Yes, that guy. Good God, I hope you're not this thick-headed when you're awake? And remember, when you do get back to me, call *this* number, not the office and definitely not the house!"

Ending the call without so much as a goodbye, Wickham stuffed the pages back into the folder. "Damn moron!" He exited his vehicle as quietly as possible and tiptoed up the deck stairs. Sliding the patio door cautiously, he slipped back into the palatial estate he and Miriam called their weekend home and poured himself the first drink of the day. He ran a few quick figures on the calculator app of his phone and, once satisfied, plopped down in the larger of the two recliners that afforded a view of the lake panorama through the massive wall of windows. His eyes scanned the water as the first light of the day illuminated its rippled surface. Through huge German-made binoculars, he surveyed the opposite shore and, one by one, mentally counted off the properties he so desperately wanted to own. "4953, 4955, 4957." He took another sip. Returning the binoculars to their case, he raised the footrest of the leather recliner and smiled. Aware that it would be another hour before Miriam stirred, the corners of his mouth curled into an evil smirk. "Those rubes won't even know what hit them." Eyes closed and hands behind his head Wickham prepared to catnap until Miriam rose to prepare his breakfast, confident that little if anything stood in his way.

Chapter 9

For as long as anybody could remember, the area between the Coffee Spot and the lake shore had been called "The Beer Garden" although it only consisted of a couple of green picnic tables "borrowed" from the nearby picnic area of the park, and little else. The locals gathered there in good weather in such consistent numbers that the bare ground underneath almost resembled a concrete patio. As for the beer, Ruthie didn't care what the occupants drank as long as they bought something from her menu. And park ranger Dalton Moore always seemed to have more pressing business than policing the gatherings of a bunch of Social Security recipients.

"Finally, we're getting some summer weather," Shirley observed.

"Frank says it's supposed to be in the 80s tomorrow," added Gloria, reaching for another handful of Ruthie's popcorn.

"Speaking of Frank, where is the old fart?" Lester asked.

"I insisted we leave the truck at home and walk over here. Thought the exercise would do him some good."

"So...Frank fell in a pot hole on the way over?"

"No! As we were passing Miss Hansen's place she was out front and asked him for some help."

"And you left him alone with her?" Shirley teased.

"Yeah, I suppose I should be worried...she's almost 90. He's always had a thing for older women."

"I wouldn't worry. I think she's a bit long in the tooth even for Frank," Lester teased.

"Speaking of Miss Hansen," Shirley inserted, "any idea what Wickham was doing poking around her place the other morning?"

"When?" asked Gloria.

"About a week ago, when you scared the crap out of me in the dark."

"Was that who almost ran you down?" Gloria asked.

"That bastard! You never told me anything about this!" Lester chided.

"He didn't even come close," Shirley assured. "But, he stopped dead in the road about where her place is and shined a light on something. And then he pulled ahead and did it again."

"That'll be two bucks," Ruthie said as she plopped an order of French fries down in front of Lester. "If you're talking about Lee Wickham, I heard the Ulrichsons took him up on his offer to buy."

"So he *is* still planning on building that hog farm!"

"Well the Ulrichsons think so; they've definitely sold their place to him...for $75,000. And yesterday, when Tucker was in, I heard him say old lady Hansen is negotiating with him too," Ruthie added as she tucked Lester's money in her apron pocket and re-entered the side door to the kitchen.

Cycling through pictures on her camera, Gloria finally broke the long silence that followed. "I wonder how much he'd give us for our place."

"Now hold on just a damned minute," Lester blurted, "you two aren't gonna let that bastard run you off, are you? We haven't even begun to fight him!"

"I just think when something like this happens, you don't want to be the last ones to the table, that's all. I was just thinking out loud." Gloria took a sip of her drink and noticed Frank coming across the parking lot. "Besides, we've got enough on our plates now."

A very tired and sweaty Frank Mariboe slowly approached the empty space at the far end of the picnic table. As he neared the others, they could see that he sported a brand new yarmulke. It also became obvious that the front of his shirt and walking shorts were covered in white powder.

"Do you have any idea how stupid you look in that?"

"Now how would I know that? I don't have a mirror!" Frank grinned.

"We waited for you," Shirley greeted, holding her half empty beer bottle up for him to see. "What happened to you?"

"Oh, on the way down I had to stop in and de-flour Miss Hansen." Puzzled looks were shared as the others tried to follow Frank's admission.

"I was cleaning up flour that spilled all over the kitchen floor," Frank explained.

"How'd that happen?" Gloria demanded.

"It got spilled while I was trying to get into her drawers..." Frank began. He was interrupted by a chorus of laughter and the sight of Lester coughing up a mouthful of beer.

"No, dammit, get your minds outta the gutter," Frank insisted. "She asked me to come in and try to free up a couple of drawers; I guess all this humidity made them stick. The first one came open pretty easy, but when I pulled on the second one, the cupboard tipped and the flour spilled all over the floor. That's all."

"So you got the flour cleaned up and the drawers open. Was she mad?" asked Shirley.

"No, she was actually grateful, 'cause she found some recipes she'd lost behind one of the drawers," Frank explained, taking his first sip of beer. "So, there was a happy ending."

At that point, Lester stood and turned away as his most recent swig of beer exited through his nose, while Shirley pounded him on the back.

"Now what'd I say?"

"Never mind, Frank," Gloria assured, "It's just Lester's dirty mind working overtime."

"You know, I was just reading the other day that men actually think of sex much more often than women do," Shirley offered, scowling at Lester. "Some men, *younger men*, claim to think about it about every ten minutes or so."

"That's bull," Lester grinned when he could talk once again. "I don't think I've ever gone that long!" This brought a good laugh from all except Shirley, who pursed her lips and continued to scowl at Lester.

Patting Frank's hand and looking him in the eye, Gloria offered, "Well, there was a time..." Her observation had a sobering effect on each of the seventy-somethings who sat silently for a while searching for a new direction for the conversation to take.

Gloria passed her camera around for everyone to look at her latest collection of sailboat photos. Before the camera reached Lester, he was drawn away by his cell phone. "Speaking...Oh hi! Brock said you'd be getting back to us." He moved away from the table a few paces. "No...I didn't know anything about a meeting. Did you try calling him?" Turning to look at his friends, Lester's brow furrowed. "No, I haven't seen him since Wednesday." Looking at his watch, he replied, "It's after five now. That was three hours ago!" Walking around the corner of the Bait Shop to where he hoped to have a view of Ashley's cabin he said, "Our place is next door to theirs, but I'm at the Bait Shop now. I can't tell from here, can't see a thing for the trees." Lester turned to go back to the others. "I'll make sure he knows the next time I see him. Next Friday at two will work for me. Sorry about the mix up. And thanks for all your help; looks like he's still planning on going ahead with it. See ya then."

Slipping his iPhone back in his pocket he made his way back to the others, intending to share the news of the call with everyone. However, it slipped his mind once he rounded the corner and saw Ashley's unmistakable form standing at the end of the table. Her long legs ended in skin-tight shorts. A tube top barely contained her ample topside. Frank's eyes were following her every move. As Lester approached the table, she turned to greet him. Her big blue eyes were red and swollen from crying as she looked up at him. "Hi Lester. Have you seen Brock today?"

"No, actually I haven't seen him for a few days now. What's up?"

"He was supposed to meet with that guy from the ICEP group today at two, but..." Her voice trailed off as the tears returned.

"Ashley?" Shirley asked, reaching up to direct her to the picnic table bench. "What is it?"

Sobbing, Ashley explained, "We had a fight yesterday. He didn't come home last night. I think it's over."

Shirley offered Ashley a napkin and put her arm around her pulling her closer. "These things happen. Have you called him?"

"I tried, but he turned his phone off. I know he hates me!" From that point on her sobbing made further communication pointless. Shirley stood and offered her more napkins. Tugging on Ashley's arm she insisted, "Come with me. I'll walk you home and you can tell me all about it. It'll all work out, you'll see."

45

Shirley's command of the situation reminded Lester of how she always handled things whenever one of their own daughter's relationships hit the rocks; she always knew just what to say. He was so thankful, as his temperament was much better suited for making the offending boy miserable than it was for soothing the hurt feelings of his own daughter.

Gloria busied herself clearing the table of empties, napkins and paper plates, while Frank sat motionless, his eyes still fixed on Ashley's shapely backside. "OK, you two, I'll run you home. I think Frank's had enough exercise for one day," Lester offered. Still no movement from the transfixed Frank Mariboe. "Frank!"

Looking back at Lester for the first time, Frank asked, "What day is it today?"

"It's Friday, June 6th. Why?"

Rising from his place at the table Frank answered, "I was just wondering how long it had been...this time."

Chapter 10

Wherever fishermen are found there are always stories about the one that got away and the fishermen of Legion Lake are no exception. But, on that rare occasion when "the big one" is actually landed or when the there's a particularly good catch, the Legion Lake Bait Shop and Coffee Spot is a fisherman's first stop after coming off the lake.

"OK, hold him up higher and smile," Ruthie ordered from the side door of the kitchen. "Or, do you need somebody to help you? This one's goin' up on the wall you know!"

Holding the nearly ten pound lunker at arm's length, Lester asked, "I get a copy, right?" Handing Ruthie his phone he added, "Here, take one on this, too! And make it quick, I gotta get Ol' Wally back in the water."

"You mean you're not going to keep him? Have him mounted?"

"Hell no, don't believe in that...a fish this big belongs in the lake!" Lester explained.

"Where's your sidekick? Frank should see this."

"They ran into town, but they should be back by now, it's almost noon." Lowering the fish back into the bucket, Lester explained, "I've gotta go show him the picture on my phone as soon as I put this guy back in." Lester lugged the heavy bucket and its precious contents down to the shore and gently released the majestic fish back into his domain. He watched until Wally disappeared from his view into the deeper water of the lake.

Once behind the wheel of his truck, he wasted no time in calling Shirley. "Hey, it's Les. I got something to show you...and Frank." He waited at the stop sign while a boy with a fishing pole over his shoulder trudged across the road ahead of him carrying his day's catch of bullheads, before turning onto the main road. "I'm on my way over there now. Be out front, I'll pick you up." Frank had hooked into Ol' Wally several times over the years, but Lester had only landed him once before. He relished the chance to even up the score a bit and perhaps make Frank feel just a bit sorry he hadn't gone with him.

He slowed to a stop on the blacktop road in front of the cabin and honked. Shirley emerged from the patio door with an apron tied around her mid-section, holding a small towel. Wiping her hands as she stepped toward the deck railing, she placed one hand on each hip and demanded, "What's so important? I just put brownies in the oven!"

"Take 'em out! And come with me. Hurry up!"

Recognizing that Lester would not take no for an answer, Shirley returned to the cabin to comply. Moments later she reemerged minus the apron and towel, but with a scowl on her face that meant Lester had better have a damn good reason for interrupting her baking. "OK, so what's so important?!"

Her tone made Lester consider for the first time that Shirley might actually be pissed at him. Retreating a bit, he apologized and started again, "I just wanted you to be with me when I show Frank," he explained reaching for her hand.

She pulled away. "This had better be good!"

"Oh trust me," he assured cautiously, "it is." He added, "And besides, we haven't been over to their place even once yet this spring. It's time we stopped in."

"If you could have waited 30 minutes, I could have brought brownies!"

Letting Shirley have the last word seemed like a good idea. As Lester pulled into the driveway, they both saw that the driver's side door of Gloria's Taurus was wide open and the motor was running. They looked at each other as Lester turned off the ignition of his truck. Without saying another word they both simultaneously reached for their respective door releases. When they reached the back door, they found it standing wide open as well. "Gloria? Are you all right?" Shirley asked through the screen.

Pulling the storm door open, Lester entered the cabin with Shirley close behind. "Frank? Gloria?"

From the bedroom Gloria answered, "I'm in here." Her voice seemed weak and her tone revealed that she was on the verge of tears.

"Where's Frank?" asked Lester, holding his phone. Shirley gave him a look that made him instantly wish he had not asked. He put his phone back in his shirt pocket.

Leaving him in the living room, she entered the bedroom alone and returned with a very dazed Gloria. Her eyes red, tear tracks on her cheeks, she sat on the couch wringing her hands. "Gloria...where's Frank?" Her only answer was a stare that could only be described as blank.

After a few seconds that seemed more like hours, Gloria finally replied, "Frank's in the hospital." Turning to make eye contact for the first time she added, "I just ran home to get him a few things."

"Oh no! What is it, pneumonia?" Shirley asked.

"They want to run some tests," she explained. Rising to her feet, the blank stare returned. "I need to get back to him."

"I don't think you should be driving; Les can take you back to town. You just sit there and try to relax while I fix you some tea."

"Is Frank all right?" Lester demanded.

"Frank's not in town. The doctor found spots on his lungs in the X-ray. They took him to the University Hospital...Iowa City. To a *cancer* specialist!" And with that, Gloria succumbed to a level of fear that no cup of tea would assuage, not even one made by Shirley.

Chapter 11

"I guess Gloria spent the night at University Hospitals in Iowa City. She just called me and asked me to let the dog out and water her houseplants. She said she'd be home tonight," Lester explained, stepping through the door. As his eyes adjusted to the relative darkness of the living room, he realized Shirley was not alone. "Oh, hi, Ashley. Any word from Brock yet?"

In spite of Lester's good intentions, his inquiry caused a torrent of sobbing to be unleashed by Ashley. While Shirley intended to do her best to console Ashley with common sense reassurance and platitudes, she knew from experience that her chances of success would not be enhanced by anything Lester added to the mix. She ushered him back through the door onto the deck and assigned him to a task sure to keep him from doing any harm to her cause. "Les, honey, why don't you be a dear and run into Casey's and pick up a pizza for supper?"

"We had pizza last night!"

Giving him a peck on the cheek she replied, "OK, then go do something else that will take you at least an hour." With that, she slid the patio door shut and locked it.

Clueless as ever about Shirley's motives, Lester climbed back into his truck and headed off to town, perhaps for burgers or maybe even a beer or two. Inside the rustic cabin, Shirley put her arm around a distraught Ashley and unfurled her own special mixture of comfort and understanding. "Can I fix you anything?"

Ashley shook her head and brushed the tears from each cheek.

"Well, I'm going to make some tea for myself then." She placed a large mug of water in the microwave and retrieved a tea bag from the cupboard. She placed the steaming mug on the table and pulled a handful of tissue from her pocket. "You really love him, don't you?"

Ashley could only nod and offer a, "Yes!" muffled by her crying.

"And he loves you as well?"

"I thought he did..."

Shirley reached for Ashley's hand and, squeezing it, offered, "These things happen between people who love each other. Lester and I have had many, many fights over the years and we just celebrated our 52nd anniversary together. He'll be back...don't you worry."

"I don't know, he was pretty mad."

Shirley sat quietly, holding her tea in one hand and Ashley's hand in the other. "Where do you think he would have gone?"

"Probably back to his roommate's apartment in Iowa City, except..."

"Except what, Ashley?"

"He doesn't own a car...he rode away on his bike."

"Well then, he couldn't have gone far," Shirley reassured. "Have you checked the campground?"

"Yes! I drove around the lake and looked for his bike. He always chains it to a tree or a light pole. I even drove around inside the campground. He's just gone, I know it!" Ashley again broke into uncontrollable sobbing.

Realizing Ashley was not going to give up the waterworks easily, Shirley switched tactics. "What did you two fight about?"

"We were talking the night before he left. Everything was great. We were having some wine and just enjoying the evening outside, when I asked him where he saw our relationship going. He just got quiet and didn't answer me."

"I see. So you broached the big question."

"Well I don't care if we get married or not, at least not right away. I just wanted to know what he intended to do after this summer. He's still got a year of college in Iowa City and then he wants to go to graduate school in California."

"Did he give any answer?"

"No. He just sat there until he finished his wine and then he got up and said he had to think and walked away."

"I thought you said he rode off on his bike?"

"He did...the next morning. Yesterday."

"So he came back from the walk?"

"About one o'clock."

"Well did he say anything then?" Shirley asked.

"Not really. I asked him where he'd been and he said he'd been walking around the lake. I was too tired to discuss it then and went to sleep."

"What did he say in the morning?"

"Nothing. He just got dressed and rode off."

Shirley considered this information and took a sip of her tea. Then she asked, "And that was yesterday morning? You haven't heard from him since then?"

"I tried calling him several times and left him three voice mails, but after that he shut off his phone."

"Well, I bet Brock is having a beer somewhere, telling his side of the story to a friend or some bartender, and slowly realizing what he has done. That always makes them come to their senses. He'll probably be home by morning."

"Do you really think so?" Ashley asked, looking up at Shirley for the first time.

"Sure!"

"But, what if he isn't?"

"Then you and I will get in my car and go drag the skunk home by the hair, the way modern cavewomen do it!"

At that, Ashley laughed out loud. "Thank you, Mrs. Pierce! You're the bomb!" Her big, blue, swollen eyes echoed the sentiment.

"Tell you what, why don't you go home and freshen up, maybe lie down a while. I'll call Lester and have him bring home enough for three. You can come back and join us for supper."

"Oh, thanks, Mrs. Pierce, but I'm not very hungry. Besides, I don't think I'd be very good company."

"It's Shirley...call me Shirley," she corrected. "Are you sure?"

"Yes, and anyway I need to make some more calls," Ashley explained, rising from her chair and moving toward the door. Hesitating only briefly, she returned and wrapped her arms around Shirley giving her a long hug. "Thanks again, Shirley. I could never have talked with my mom like this. She hates Brock." With that, she headed out the door.

Shirley wondered about Brock and about Ashley. She wondered if she had said the right things. Had she helped Ashley or simply prolonged the inevitable? Where was Brock and how long would it take him to come to his senses? These questions and many others went through her mind as she watched Ashley walk back to the little red cabin. But one thing she did know for sure – if these two didn't get it together soon, it would be a *long* summer. Having been there once already with her own daughter, Shirley was certain of that.

Chapter 12

"Are you sure you want to do this? Couldn't you call the guy and postpone it again?" Shirley questioned.

"I already told you, we have to keep fighting this until Wickham gives it up!" Lester opened a manila folder containing receipts, handwritten notes, emails and pages with the header, Legion Lake Aquatic Samples, "Are you sure this is everything?"

"Ashley said she looked through his workspace twice and put all his papers in that folder."

"Well, I wish I'd paid more attention in biology class. I don't have a clue what most of this stuff means. I hope the guy from ICEP can decipher it. It'd sure be nice of that little jerk to come back and finish what he started!"

"I don't know when that will happen. I'm worried about Ashley. I encourage her to keep her hopes up, but it's been two weeks. I'm sure wherever he's holed up, he'll come back someday soon for his things. And Ashley says his mail is still coming, bills and such."

"Well, that's a good sign isn't it? I mean if he doesn't intend to return, he'd have had his mail forwarded at least by now," Lester observed.

Unconvinced, Shirley continued. "Maybe. If and when that happens...then it'll be over officially between them. Until then, I'll try to support her, but..."

"I don't get it. He was so into fighting this thing, he collected all this data and then he just...blew town? Over a lover's spat? What a jerk!" Lester fastened a large binder clip over the folder and retrieved a pen and a pad of paper from the desk drawer.

"Aren't you coming with me? It's almost two."

"No, I need to go over to Gloria's and check on her garden, see if the yard needs mowing. These trips to Iowa City for Frank's treatments haven't left them much time to be here. I hope somebody's helping take care of their place in Grinnell."

"OK, but I gotta head out then. You know Shirley Pierce, you're really a nice person. A good friend." With that he gave her a peck on the cheek and added, "Wish me luck."

"You're a pretty nice guy yourself, mister. Heading up this fight for the whole lake."

Lester turned at the door to look at her. "That's nice of you to say. Sort of sounds like you're flirting with me, Mrs. Pierce." The corner of Shirley's mouth turned up in a wry little smile. "If you're not busy later when I get home..." Shirley grabbed the pillow from the couch and threw it at Lester as the door closed behind him.

As he drove down the blacktop road that led into town, Lester couldn't help thinking about Brock. He really hoped that Brock would be waiting at the café' along with Charlie Grisham from the ICEP, and that he would have more information for them to use to fight Wickham's idiotic plan. That's what he wanted to believe, but he was pretty sure that Brock wouldn't show. *Just like one of those college boys, first time things get rough they cut and run,* he thought. What he couldn't understand was how any guy could stay away so long over a quarrel. Maybe he wasn't mad at Ashley so much as afraid of what she wanted to do to him. An unexpected marriage proposal from a guy's girlfriend could be a terrifying thing. Not that Lester had even come close to such an experience – he had to ask Shirley three times before she agreed to marry him. He'd never had much luck attracting women. In fact, in high school he was known as something of an expert at *repelling* the opposite sex. No, Lester hadn't actually had such an experience, but he could relate just the same.

He was relieved to see so many empty parking spaces in front of the City Café. There was a good chance their meeting could be held in relative privacy. He wasn't at all sure what Mr. Grisham would have to say – or Brock either if he showed his face – but the fewer people who overheard their conversation, the better. Once he was inside and his eyes had adjusted to the dim light, he realized his optimism had been unjustified – the place was half-full of two o'clock coffee drinkers. The seed corn cap wearing variety who had nothing better to do but sit forever and pass on the latest gossip or, worse yet, soak up new information to disseminate over tomorrow's cup of java. To his relief,

Lester spotted an outlier, dressed in shorts and a polo shirt, sitting alone at the counter next to a worn leather pouch.

"Charlie?" he asked tentatively as he extended his hand.

"You must be Lester," the man affirmed. "Brock's not with you?"

"No, I hope he'll be joining us, but I'm not sure."

"I guess I don't understand..." Charlie replied.

"Has he been in contact with you?"

"No. Not for a few weeks. I left him a voicemail about today's meeting. I told him to call me back if he couldn't make it, but he didn't," Charlie explained as he checked his phone. "Nope, no new messages. Why wouldn't he be here?"

Noticing that the old guys in the nearest booth were all watching them, Lester motioned to the waitress. "Let's find a table."

"Where would you gentlemen like to sit? And what can I get you?"

"We just need to have a quiet place to discuss some business," Lester explained. "Is there another room?"

"Just the dining room, but we don't open that until 5:30."

"Charlie, can I buy you some coffee and pie?"

Still looking a bit puzzled, Charlie accepted. "Sure, unleaded, black and apple if you've got it."

"OK, I'll have the same," Lester told the waitress. "And if you could serve us that in the dining room, we promise to keep the door shut and not tell anyone." He handed the waitress a five-dollar bill, thanking her for the extra trouble.

Smiling, she accepted the bribe and explained, "I'm sure I can work something out. The dining room is through that door and the light switch is on the left."

As they headed into the dining room, Charlie asked, "OK, so what's with Brock?"

"I'm not sure. I was afraid he might not show, so I got his data from his girlfriend," he answered waving the manila folder in his hand.

"That surprises me. He seemed like such a responsible young man."

"I know, but..." Lester stopped short as the waitress entered the room with a tray.

"Here's your coffee and pie, and I added a scoop of ice cream."

"At no charge," she whispered to Lester. "Will there be anything else?"

"No, just leave us in here to talk and that will be it. Thank you! Oh, there is one other thing. If a young man with long hair and a beard comes in, send him in. We're expecting him, his name's Brock."

"Brock Sanford?"

"Yes. Do you know him?"

"Not well. He used to come in a couple of times a week and ask for a latte. Nice guy. Cute! But I haven't seen him for a couple of weeks. Ashley either." She picked up the tray and laid the check in front of Lester, turning to smile at him as she pulled the door shut on her way out of the dining room.

"You were saying?"

"Well, Brock lives with his girlfriend out at the lake, and it seems she raised the question of marriage, and..." Lester motioned and shrugged, smiling ever so slightly.

Charlie took a moment to consider the information and then offered, "He bolted?"

"Like a jack rabbit!"

"When?"

"Just before the first meeting you had scheduled. He's either scared out of his mind or insane."

"Insane?"

"He's nuts if you ask me. A nerd like him isn't likely to get another shot at a great girl like Ashley."

"I see. And you haven't heard from him for more than two weeks then? Well, I suppose we might as well move on. Can I see his data?"

Charlie removed the binder clip and looked through the folder, reading each page as he went. When he finally looked up, he asked, "Have you looked at this?"

"Well, yeah, sort of. Why?"

"Almost everything in here has to do with pollution already *in* your lake; E. coli O157:H7 to be exact."

"Yeah. so..."

"When I first talked to Brock he said he was gathering baseline data on air quality, silt, runoff, aquatic life, and so on. A host of data that could be used to describe the current condition of the lake environment as well as point out the likely ways in which the environment would be susceptible to the impact of Wickham's CAFO. All this tells me is that Brock found a high level of E. coli pollution *already* present in the lake."

Lester's brow furrowed as he asked, "Are you sure?"

"I have a Ph.D. and 30 years of experience in environmental research. I'm one of those 'nerds' you referred to. Yes, I'm sure!"

"Why would he tell you he was doing all that if he wasn't?"

"I'm not saying he lied. I'm saying that *this* data can't be everything he was gathering. There has to be more somewhere…a lot more."

"But Ashley looked through all his things at their cabin and this was it."

"Well, if I was him, I wouldn't have let it out of my sight. He probably has it with him." Charlie pulled his phone out and placed a call. "I'm calling him again to see if he's on his way." He let it ring until it went to voicemail and then, with no small amount of frustration, he left a message, "Brock this is Charlie. Lester and I have been waiting on you for ten minutes. I don't know what you're doing, but if you want my help from the ICEP group, you're gonna have to get your shit together! I need your data! Call me, and let me know what's going on. If I don't hear from you by Monday, I'll have no choice but to close your file and move on."

Lester shook his head slowly and looked up from his pie at Charlie. "Is that it? You're just gonna drop us like that?"

"Mr. Pierce, I won't have any choice. I have dozens of these cases to assist with this summer. Because of the way the legislature has weakened the laws in Iowa in recent years, it's nearly impossible to fight a CAFO as it is and, without Brock's data, I'll have absolutely nothing to go on. I'm not about to square off with county supervisors or the DNR with only a smile on my face. This is my second trip out here only to be stood up by Brock." He looked down at the untouched pie on his plate and the cup of coffee. "That pie any good?"

"It's not bad. The coffee helps choke it down. So what can I do to keep this alive? Surely there's more to fighting the CAFO than the lake data?"

Charlie took a bite of the pie and followed it up with a swig of coffee. "Pie's too sweet. Good apple pie is made with green apples." Once he had finished his second bite he leaned forward and looked Lester in the eye. "Look, I don't mean to be a hard-ass. I'm just telling it like it is. Brock has the data I need to make a convincing presentation to the supervisors and the DNR. Without it, I'd just be wasting everybody's time."

"Well, what can we do...the residents of the lake? Isn't there anything else that can be done besides your presentation to the county and the state?"

Charlie took another bite of pie and looked around the room as he formed an answer. "Brock said Wickham had bought an option on the land. Find out if he actually closed on it yet." Charlie reached into his leather pouch and pulled out two pages with the Iowa DNR symbol at the top. "Here are the steps anyone has to take to acquire all the permissions necessary to operate a CAFO. At the very least, you can check to see how far he's gotten. In this, like everything else, knowledge is power."

Lester took the pages and, after a cursory look, realized he understood very little of what was before him. "Maybe we should hire a lawyer and sue the bastard?"

"You could, but that's what *we'll* do at ICEP...once we get the data together, and any lawyer would need the same things I requested from Brock. I'm sorry, but I can't make any meaningful progress with this case until I get Brock's data. Find him and get him to fork it over. In the meantime, check out where Wickham's at in the process."

As Charlie cleaned up the last of his pie, Lester looked over the DNR pages again, cursing under his breath. Stacking his pie plate, cup and fork in a tidy little pile, Charlie added, "That ranger...Dalton? He should be able to help you check out that list. If anyone out at the lake would be knowledgeable about the process, it would be him. And Wickham of course." Snapping the clasp on the leather pouch, Charlie rose from his chair and pushed it back under the table. "Well, good luck, Mr. Pierce. You're gonna need it if you don't get Brock's data." With that he turned and added, "Thanks for the coffee and pie," as he headed for the door.

"I'll call you again as soon as Brock shows his face," Lester yelled, but Charlie was already out of the dining room and out of earshot. Lester sat staring at the DNR papers, picking at his pie. As he read through the list of requirements, he tried to imagine how Wickham would make his way through them and the answer boiled down to two things – money and power. He knew Wickham had plenty of both and that he had probably turned the whole process over to his attorney who had made quick work of it.

In an uncharacteristic move, Lester turned the pages over and began to make a list, a plan actually. He wrote down everything he could think of that would help with the problem. Then he made another list of specific things that would require Dalton's help. He studied his plan and took a swig of his now cold coffee. Suddenly, he wadded up the page, crushed it into a ball and threw it as far as he could across the dining room. On the back of the second paper he started another list – a list of all the improvements he and Shirley had made to their property over the years and the dollar amounts associated with each. At the bottom, he wrote the purchase price of the cabin in 1980: $45,000. It totaled up to a sum just over $100,000. And that didn't account for all the "sweat equity" they had invested. He had no idea what the market value was, but he felt certain any offer Wickham made wouldn't come close to being enough. He folded the paper and tucked it into his wallet. He stared at the half-eaten pie which he had no desire to finish. Lester Pierce was normally not a man who ran from a tough job or who gave up easily. But, for the moment, he was tempted to do both.

Chapter 13

"Goddamn it," Lester said aloud. No sooner had the words left his mouth than he regretted yelling. Suddenly, he appreciated the fact that he was alone in the dining room and that the door was closed. Rising from his chair, he took the bill and started for the door, but made a wide loop across the room and retrieved the wadded up DNR paper, which he folded and stuffed into his shirt pocket. He emerged from the dining room and left the bill and ten dollars on the register without a word to the waitress.

The drive back to the lake gave him some time to cool off, but it didn't provide an answer to the most troublesome question: What should he say to Shirley about their future at the lake? As much as he hated the thought of selling out after all their hard work, he knew she would be absolutely crushed if they had to give up their place. He thought about the plans they had made before they retired and how they both assumed that summers at the lake would be a part of their life as long as they were physically able. He tried to imagine fishing, or cruising the lake on the pontoon once Wickham's pig farm was in full swing. As he thought of a barbeque on the deck accompanied by the aroma of hog manure, it was all he could do to keep down the pie and coffee. But the thought of selling their property, possibly to Wickham, was just as sickening.

As he rounded the last corner before the entrance to Legion Lake Park, the late afternoon sun burned through the side window and made him regret once again that he had not sprung for tinted glass when he bought his truck. He grabbed the visor and turned it to the side releasing the stash of important papers he kept above it. He grabbed at the ensuing avalanche, while doing his best to maintain control of the vehicle. Out of the corner of his eye, he became aware of something moving directly toward the road from his right. Slamming on the brakes, he slid to a stop just as a boy on a bike dashed across the road in front of him and disappeared onto the bike path through the woods. "Damned kid!" Lester shouted. "You could've been killed!" For a moment he just sat there, cussing the boy, all the while aware that it was he who should have been more careful. Finally, checking the mirror for any traffic behind him and finding none, he gathered the assortment of building center receipts, maps, vehicle registration and notes written to himself and tried to organize them for their return to the visor where they would await the next avalanche event. When he came across the notice to pay the property taxes on the cabin, he cussed again, realizing the payment was past due. Knowing this would mean not only a substantial late fee, but a trip into the court house, he again turned to the vast collection of swear words in his vocabulary to express his frustration. But, he stopped before vocalizing a single one when it occurred to him that any filings Wickham had already made would be at the same court house. He immediately saw a silver lining. He could explain the trip into the county seat to Shirley as a bold attempt on his part to fight the Wickham mess and not mention the belated tax payment. *Yes, I might just dodge this bullet after all.*

The fact that he now had at least the beginnings of a plan helped reduce his anger, as well as his blood pressure, and he noticed a growing feeling of confidence as he neared the cabin. *Yes! I'll drive to the courthouse tomorrow morning, pay the taxes and find out how far Wickham has taken his idiotic plan. This will be O.K.*

Chapter 14

Frank's Tacoma was still in the drive as he passed Mariboe's, but Gloria's car was gone, which told Lester that it must be a treatment day for Frank. Everything else at the lake appeared as it should be on a summer afternoon – quiet, peaceful, absolutely no indication of the impending havoc which was sure to threaten the entire area if Wickham got his way with the CAFO. The only other vehicle on the road was the power company truck he met on the way to his own little piece of heaven. Once the truck passed him, it slowed and turned around in Frank's drive, eventually catching up to Lester as he turned into his own drive. The man behind the wheel exited the vehicle and quickly approached Lester.

"Afternoon. My name's Groves, Ed Groves. I'm the site supervisor for the wind farm 21st Century's putting in south of here. I'm looking for an employee, or former employee, named Brock Sanford. He live around here anywhere?"

Lester pointed to the red cabin and offered simply, "Used to. Flew the coop over two weeks ago."

"You mean he took off? Well that's just great! Now what the hell am I supposed to do?"

"I don't know what to tell you. He left us in a rather bad spot too."

"Owe you money did he?"

"No, but we were counting on him to provide some environmental data we need to..." Lester decided the power company didn't need to know about Brock's involvement with problems at the lake.

"Well, the reports he was working on and never filed have ground a project worth several million to a halt. If I don't find him and get that information filed, there will be hell to pay.

"You could talk to his girlfriend Ashley, but I don't think she knows any more about his whereabouts than anybody else. It looks like he just had enough and decided to take off."

"That's just great! God damned kid! I never trusted him. What'd you say her name is?" he asked, motioning in the direction of the red cabin.

"Ashley. Ashley Edwards. She's probably home."

"Thanks." Groves climbed the steps to Ashley's cabin like a man on a mission and pounded on the door.

I'd sure hate to be Brock when he catches up to him, he thought as he parked his truck. Construction workers with deadlines and multiple contractors weren't known for their patience and tended to charge in first and let the excuses come later.

That thought jolted Lester back into his own reality and the mission he had been on – paying the property taxes on the cabin without letting Shirley find out he'd let them slide. He entered the cabin whistling, his eyes scanning the living room for Shirley's purse and the checkbook it contained, but he found no sign of it. "Hi, hon, I'm back."

"I'm in the bedroom on the computer. How'd it go? Was Brock there?"

"No, the little turd didn't show again and it didn't go well at all. The guy from the ICEP said the data Ashley found won't help our cause and more or less washed his hands of us until I can produce Brock's data. That's gonna be hard to do unless he shows his face again."

"So that's it. We're just supposed to give up?"

"No, he gave me a list of things to check out about Wickham and the property, but we'll definitely need the data if we have to actually fight him in a hearing. I'm actually on my way now into the court house to start the search. I need the checkbook, you know in case there's charges or fees."

Shirley reached in the closet for her purse and retrieved the checkbook. But before releasing her grip on it, she laid out her usual conditions, "Make sure you enter *every* check you write in the register and write the amount so I can *read* it!"

"Yes, dear."

"And while you're in there, stop at the Treasurer's Office and pay the property taxes."

Lester's expression confirmed that he knew he was busted. All he could muster was a simple, "But how..."

"First of all, I don't see any entry for that check in the register. And second, the delinquency notice came weeks ago, but with all this upheaval about Wickham...well, I forgot to nag you."

"You forgot? Now I have to pay late fees and..."

"Don't push it, buster!"

Realizing he'd already blown by the exit for the high road, he took the checkbook from her hand and said simply, "OK, gotta run before they close."

* * *

The drive gave him plenty of time to organize his request for information about Wickham, but by the time he arrived at the court house it was 3:30, leaving him only a half hour before they closed. Although he wanted to delay paying the taxes a few more minutes and start digging on Wickham's project, he peered into the Treasurer's Office. Seeing no line, he walked up to the counter, checkbook in hand. It was at that moment that he realized he had no clue where to begin investigating Wickham anyway. "I need to pay my property taxes."

A middle-aged woman with silver hair seated at a desk in the back of the room looked at him over her glasses and replied, "Yes you do. We *all* do. And they were due back in March."

Lester wasn't sure whether she was attempting to be funny or just outright snarky – either way he was in no mood. "I know that. We *all* know that. And I'm here now to pay them," he explained waving his checkbook.

Looking every bit as though walking to the counter to accept his check represented a huge favor to Lester, she slowly rose from her chair and moved in his direction. "Tax statement?"

Lester handed her the original statement as well as the past due notice Shirley had given him. She took both and returned to her desk where she opened a thick binder of computer printouts and leafed through them. Finally she scrawled a figure on a note pad, tore off the page and returned to the counter, handing it to Lester. Her scrawl read "$955 tax plus $72 late fee." The printing at the top of the note read, "Pat Lloyd, County Treasurer - Service With a Smile."

Groaning, he wrote a check for $1,027. As he passed it to her along with his list from Charlie, he asked, "Could you tell me which office would have this information?"

Retrieving a pencil from the nest of gray hair atop her head and fetching her glasses from the chain around her neck, she ran down the list making a clicking sound as she made imaginary check marks next to each item. "These are all related to building a CAFO," she informed.

"Yes, I know that, but which office would have information about who owns the property it's being built on?"

"Oh, well property transfer documents are all in the Recorder's Office on the third floor."

"OK, thank you very much...Pat," Lester said after checking her name tag. He turned and moved quickly out the door, thinking that there must be two "Pats" that work in the Treasurer's Office. He moved up the stairs at a pace more rapid it turned out, than his overall condition would support. By the time he found the Recorder's Office and pulled open the huge door, he was winded and took a couple of beats before he answered the young woman's inquiry of, "How can I help you?"

He showed her his list and explained that he wanted to know who owned the property on 280th Ave. After less than a minute at her keyboard, she announced, "It's recorded under the names of Tomas F. and Alice E. Wallace of the same address."

"What about the option? Do you show an option on the property by a man named Wickham? Lee Wickham?"

"No, but options are simply an agreement between the owner and an interested buyer to sell the property by a particular date. They aren't actual transfers of property, so they aren't recorded in our office."

Looking at the clock, Lester pleaded, "Where are they recorded?"

"That's just it, I don't think they're required to be recorded." Picking up on his frustration, she explained further, "Look, I'm just the Recorder's assistant and I've only been on the job a few months. The Recorder has already left. Tell me what you're trying to find, and I'll ask her to call you with answers when she returns."

Thinking he'd finally hit some pay dirt, Lester explained his overall mission and that he needed to know how far Wickham had gone with the purchase of the property, DNR permits, etc.

"Well I know DNR permits come through this office, bu, again, Dorothy handles those. I don't even know where they're filed. But if you'll write down the name and address of this 'Wickham' fellow, I'll ask Dorothy to check for permits as soon as she returns."

"You mean tomorrow?"

"No, I'm sorry, but she left today for California. Her mother passed last night and, between the services and wrapping up the estate, there's no telling when she'll be back at work. But I'll make certain she gets this and I'll be sure to emphasize how badly you want the information." Seeing her smile, Lester found the strength to refrain from expressing his disappointment. Then she asked, "What's a CAFO anyway?"

"A confined animal feeding operation, in this case a hog confinement."

"Oooooh! I'll make *certain* she gets back to you!"

"I know you will. And thanks for all your help."

Lester left the courthouse with a checkbook, a receipt for past due property taxes and very little else. Except the promise that the Recorder would call him in maybe two weeks. Something told him that, the assistant would make sure she did.

Chapter 15

The rising sun revealed a cloudless sky that foretold a scorcher, and the thermometer confirmed it. Lester's watch read 5:27 a.m. when he rose to answer his final duty call of the night, and it was already 83 degrees outside. In the breaking light of dawn, he could see evidence of the storm that had howled on through the night and the power to the cabin still had not returned. His lawn was now littered with small twigs and leaves he would dispatch the next time he mowed and larger limbs and branches he would be removing as soon as Shirley noticed them. Even without checking, he knew the rain gauge was nearly full, because of the deep ruts washed out in the gravel driveway. Yes, his day was already looking full and he hadn't even had his first cup of coffee.

Lester despised days like this, days that started out with temps in the high 80s and humidity even higher. He could tell this one would be at least a three-shirter. He knew he would be clearing debris and hauling loads to the dump pile most of the day. And the only relief in sight from either the heat or the work would be to escape onto the water. And that wouldn't happen until he had dealt with Shirley's ever growing list of clean-up jobs. It's a wise man who meets his fate head on. Lester, on the other hand, made a pot of "fisherman's coffee" on the gas stove and poured a large mug for himself. With no electricity to power the TV, he slipped out onto the deck to experience what likely would be the least uncomfortable hour of the day. The flooded flower pots on the deck rail confirmed that the lake had received heavy rain over night.

Across the water on the far shore, no lights marked the larger cabins, a sign that even the properties of the wealthy weren't immune to the storm's effects. He moved to the very edge of the deck and stretched over the railing, craning his neck to look down the blacktop road to the east toward Frank and Gloria's place. No signs of life were apparent in that direction, but he became aware of the growing sound of a vehicle approaching from the other way. Seconds later he saw the single headlight that was the trademark of Frank Mariboe's Tacoma on high beam. Working his way down the driveway, he stood in the dim light until Frank was close enough to see him.

"How much rain did we get? Or was it mainly blow?"

"My gauge says four inches, and I believe it the way the lake is up," answered Frank.

"Where ya been at this hour?"

"In town to Casey's to get a thermos of coffee."

"Hell, I've got coffee. You could've come over here for a cup."

"That stuff you call coffee? No, thanks! I prefer the real thing, and I wanted a paper."

"Probably a couple of donuts, I suspect."

"Probably," Frank answered with a smile, holding up the plastic bag of pastries.

"But even donuts don't explain the smile on your face. What's up?"

Leaning through the open window, Frank broadened his smile into a full grin and made a beckoning motion, saying only, "Get in!"

Recognizing a spark in his old friend he hadn't seen in many weeks, Lester gladly obliged. "What's up, bud?" he asked eagerly as he climbed into the Frank's truck and shut the door.

"Well, you know the kid who clerks at Casey's in the mornings?"

"Pimple-faced Ron?"

"Yeah, but you really need to cut him some slack. He gave me a great tip."

"A fishing tip?"

"Nope! Way better than that! He says word around town is that there's a group of hotties who plan to go skinny dipping out here at the beach...tonight!"

"You gotta be kidding. Who are they?"

"He didn't say, just that they were locals."

"So how does he know this?"

"He overheard them talking about it when they were buying gas."

Lester mulled the bulletin over a bit and then asked, "So what's this supposed to do for us?"

"He said they were planning on going in as soon as it gets dark. We go out on your pontoon at dusk and float by the beach and enjoy the view. Maybe hit the lights and give 'em a scare. Come on, it'll be a hoot!"

"Yeah? And what do we tell the wives? 'Oh, Frank and I are just going for a little cruise in the moonlight?' "

"That's the beauty of it. Tonight's the girls' annual night out. You know, Gloria's been talking about it all week! Last year the four of them went to Iowa City for a movie and dinner, and they didn't come home until after midnight."

A wry smile slowly appeared on Lester's face as he pulled on the door lever. "Well then, you better get home and get your storm cleanup done. I'll need your help to get the lights and horn working on the pontoon!"

"Way ahead of you, Les. I stopped at NAPA and picked up this spotlight. As long as your lighter outlet works, we're in business."

As Lester exited the Tacoma, he marveled at the fact that Frank's libido still functioned at all let alone at this level. *Oh well*, he thought to himself. *I guess he's still got it!* But somewhere in the back of his mind Lester knew that all either he or Frank really had was the ability to fool themselves into thinking they still 'had it.'

As he eased back down onto the bench on the deck, he drained the last gulp of coffee from his cup with a grimace – Frank might be right about his coffee. Although the sun had just cleared the tops of the trees between him and the eastern horizon, the rhythmic clank of Ryan Benson's diesel truck starting told Lester it was already six o'clock. In all the years he and Shirley had been at the lake, he had never known Ryan to fail to be on the road by six a Lester reasoned that he might as well be working on the storm clean-up when Shirley got up. If she caught him at work before she had to nag, it might translate to valuable brownie points later on. Points he might well need if she got wind of the little moonlight voyage he and Frank planned that evening.

By 7:30, Lester was finishing with the last load of branches when he noticed the porch light on the rental was lit. As he stepped onto his deck he could hear the morning news and knew Shirley was up for the day and that the power was back on. Channel 9 was reporting that the night's storms had covered a wide area of Iowa and that rainfall ranged from two to four inches. He trudged down the bank to the shore where he confirmed that the lake level was considerably higher than the day before. Frank had been right about the rainfall. Lester hoped his other bit of news was just as accurate.

As he returned to the cabin, he took note of the small twigs and leaves that littered the lawn. He quickly dispatched them with the rider and doing so gave the impression that he was mowing ahead of schedule, something that would also translate to more points with Shirley. Once that was done, all that remained would be a few trips to the gravel pile for enough rock to repair the wash outs. And that could wait until after breakfast.

As he entered the cabin, Shirley was just serving up his breakfast of scrambled eggs and whole wheat toast. "Morning, Dear," he greeted her as he gave her a peck on the cheek.

Somewhat taken aback, she pulled away and asked, "Morning to you too...everything all right?"

"Sure is! Can't I give my wife a kiss?"

"Yes...you just surprised me, that's all."

"So what's on your schedule for today?"

Again glaring at him in surprise she replied, "The usual I guess. Make your lunch, lay in the shade and read, make you dinner. You know, living the dream." She took a sip of coffee and picked away at her own breakfast. They both ate quietly, staring at the lake through the picture window.

Eventually she asked, "How about you?"

"I need to finish cleaning up from the storm, fix the driveway wash outs. Then I thought I would work on the old tub some more. You know the storm washed in a lot of trash and raised the lake at least a foot. I think I'd better make sure all the equipment is working. With all the debris in the lake, it would be just like Dalton to start doing safety checks."

"Oh, what's the matter with me, I won't be home tonight! The girls and I are having our movie and dinner night in Iowa City, so you'll have to make your own dinner."

"That's tonight? Well, don't worry about me, maybe Frank and I can go into town for pizza. We'll get along, you girls just have fun. What's the movie you're going to see?"

"Um, I'm not sure, it's something Shirley's friend recommended, and I think it's what you'd call a chick flick".

"Figures. Thanks for sparing me." Lester popped the last bite of toast in his mouth and tossed back the last of his coffee. As he made his way to the sink with his dishes, he swooped in on Shirley's neck and gave her one more kiss. "And thanks for making me breakfast!"

Wiping off her neck and pulling away, Shirley's lips started to form a protest, but slowly turned to a smile as Lester went out the patio door whistling.

By 9:15, Lester had hauled the second load of gravel to fill in the ruts in the driveway. Once he had driven over it a few times and pulled the drag over it with the rider, it was good as new. With that job behind him, he loaded tools, electrical wire and tape into his tool box and headed for his dock. After clearing leaves and branches from the deck of the pontoon, he punched in the cigarette lighter. Within ten seconds it popped out as expected, red hot, proving that there was current. He flipped on the running side lights and stern light, but no such luck. One by one, he tightened the wire connectors for each light and carefully wrapped each connection with electrical tape. Eventually, his efforts paid off as all three lights shined brightly the next time he tried them. Satisfied with his efforts, he retrieved the gas can from the shed and made sure the tank on the pontoon was filled. Holding his hand over his brow, he glanced in the direction of the sun. It looked to be close to eleven.

Unaccustomed as he was to working such a long, uninterrupted stretch in such heat and humidity, he was not at all surprised that his shirt was totally soaked with sweat. Making one final check of the life preservers under the seats, he gathered his tools and the gas can and headed back to the yard. As soon as the tools and can were back in the shed, he took a much-deserved break in the hammock under the big maple tree. He told himself he would rest his eyes for a few minutes and then go in for some lunch.

His thoughts turned to his friend, Frank, who still had enough spunk to suggest the escapade they had planned for the evening despite his cancer and treatment. The same Frank who had helped him build the deck, paint the cabin and even plant the very tree in the shade of which he now rested. He couldn't imagine what all the years at the lake would have been like without his friendship with Frank and Gloria.

Sounds coming from within his cabin told him Shirley was preparing his lunch. He knew he should go in, but the slight breeze coming off the lake combined with the dampness of his shirt was too comforting to abandon. His thoughts turned into dreams as he drifted off into one of his spontaneous naps.

"Les? What're you doing? You OK?" Shirley asked from the open patio door. "I put your sandwich and salad back in the fridge."

"What? Um, I'm coming in. I was just cooling off a bit first."

"You did more than cool off. You've been in that hammock for an hour and a half. What were you doing to wear yourself out so?"

Pulling himself up into a standing position, Lester bought some time before explaining himself. "I've been working on the boat, trying to fix some of the things Frank's always bitching about when we're out fishing. You'd think he was a DNR ranger the way he picks away at her shortcomings."

"Well, good for him. That gives *both* of you something to do," Shirley teased. "Wouldn't want anything to happen to my boys while they were out on the lake tormenting the fish, now would I?"

"Don't worry about that. She may not be pretty, but with those foam-filled logs, she's as unsinkable as the Titanic!"

Shirley turned, placed her hands on her hips and glared at him in disbelief.

"You know what I mean!" Pulling his sweat-soaked shirt over his head he tossed it in the laundry basket on his way to the bedroom to retrieve a clean one. From the bedroom he asked, "So where you ladies going tonight?"

"Into Iowa City for a little shopping, then dinner and a movie. Same as always."

"Sounds like fun. I guess I can scare up something in town and then watch the tube until bedtime. Probably still be too damned hot to be outside. Might turn in early, try not to wake me when you get back. Take your phone, you know, just in case."

"The four of us can take care of ourselves. We do this every year. And you know we won't be home before midnight, so don't wait up."

Lester emerged from the bedroom sporting his favorite 'work' shirt, a gray, well-ventilated jersey tee with a large grease spot on the stomach. "I thought I threw that thing in the trash!"

"You did. I pulled it out just in time. The garbage guy almost had it."

"You stubborn old fart. You know I hate that thing on you. Makes you look homeless."

"It's comfortable and I can work in it without worrying about ruining it." Lester settled into his recliner with his sandwich and a can of beer and reached for the remote. Shirley took the satisfied grin on his face to mean that he had once again won the battle over his favorite shirt, but for Lester it reflected something entirely different.

Chapter 16

The sudden cold, wet sensation on his leg woke Lester from his second spontaneous nap of the day. The beer he had been nursing during the first few minutes of the mid-afternoon offering on the Western Channel had finally teetered over into his lap just as the credits were scrolling up the screen. "Damn it!" He futilely brushed away at the beer soaking into the leg of his shorts. Releasing the lever of the recliner, he returned it to the upright position and stood up. "Shirley?" he called out. The half sheet of paper he then noticed sailing away from his chest told him there would be no answer. Retrieving it from its resting place under the TV stand he read Shirley's note.

> We're heading out for Iowa City now. Should be back around midnight. Take Frank into town with you for supper. I didn't kiss you goodbye because I could see you were hard at it in your "work shirt!" See you tonight (or tomorrow), you old fart! - Love, Shirley.

Dumbfounded that he could have slept through an entire western including the commercials, he checked his phone and, sure enough, the time read 4:17. "Holy crap!" he uttered. But he quickly rationalized that, given the combination of heat, humidity, his heavy lunch and the beer, a lesser man would still be sawing logs. And, since he and Frank had a late night ahead of them, the long nap was actually a good investment.

He checked the kitchen for the provisions their nighttime outing would require. He found a full 12-pack of bottled water and two beers in the fridge. A search of the cupboards turned up a couple dozen homemade chocolate chip cookies and full box of Twinkies. He retrieved the ice chest from the basement, but, finding no sign of ice in the freezer, he gave Frank a call. "Yeah, Frank? Hot enough for you? Are we still on for tonight?"

Frank confirmed his continued interest.

"Let's get out on the water before sunset so we won't have to leave the dock in the dark. There's a full moon tonight so coming back in should be doable...if you remember your spotlight. I got the lighter socket working again. And all the running lights."

Addressing his more immediate needs, Frank asked, "You got plans for supper?"

"Yeah, I plan on picking you up in about an hour and goin' into town for burgers or pizza." The pause that followed signaled the cellular version of the customary standoff over picking up the tab. Being in dire need to pay the rent on the beer he consumed earlier, Lester made the first move. "You got any ice?"

The seemingly unrelated question threw Frank temporarily into suspicion. "Yeah...just bought a fifteen-pound bag yesterday. Why?"

"Cause we're out and we'll need some tonight. You bring the ice and supper's on me."

"Deal!"

Once inside the bathroom, Lester was forced to take stock of himself as he passed the mirror and did not like what he saw...or smelled. He made room in his schedule for a shower and a change into clean, presentable clothes. No telling who he might run into in town. By five o'clock, he was presentable again – by his own standards if not Shirley's. Before heading out the door, he found Shirley's note and added his response, just in case she returned early.

>Will do! After supper Frank and I are
>going out fishing. Back at ya! Lester

By 6:15, he and Frank had finished off a large pie at the Pizza Palace, half-sausage and half-anchovy. Frank would have preferred his half covered in lutefisk, but anchovies were an acceptable substitution. Lester picked up the check and, to save time, told Frank, "The $2.50 tip's on you." Frank complied by only rolling of his eyes once.

"Thanks for supper. So now what you wanna do?"

"What time did the kid tell you the girls were supposed to be skinny-dipping?"

"He didn't really nail the time down, just after dark was all."

"Well, that gives us about three hours to kill. I guess we could drive around and see what's shaking in town."

"Yeah, I guess."

Lester rose and slid his chair back under the table. As he turned toward the register to pay the bill, he motioned again for Frank to pony up the tip which he grudgingly did. After giving Lester a good looking over, the young man running the till observed, "Haven't seen you fellas in here before. Your first time at Pizza Palace?"

"We're from out at the lake and don't dine out often. Our wives are out of town, so we were looking for a meal we didn't have to make ourselves."

"Well, come back soon and bring the ladies with you next time."

"We'll be sure to do that," Lester lied, having no intention of returning.

"Just a minute, I gotta make a pit stop," Frank interrupted.

Lester helped himself to a couple of mints and headed out the door. In the 45 minutes they had been inside the pizza joint, the temperature had only dropped a few degrees, but the humidity was much better and a nice breeze could be felt. The crickets were already tuning up, their only competition was the occasional passing car as one of the local heartthrobs scooped the loop. This was what Iowa small town life had always been; he saw no good reason why it shouldn't be that way forever, although he felt certain it would not.

Frank emerged from the Pizza Palace ready to go. "Hey, you heard any more about Wickham's crazy ideas?"

"Nothing since the last time I filled you in." Lester headed for his truck with Frank in tow.

"What about Brock? Do you think he'll ever come back and help us?"

Lester backed the truck out and started down the street. "I think he's long gone, either shacked up with another woman or more likely, he's stooped over a batch of pond scum samples making love to his data!"

"I suppose. Seems kinda weird that he'd go off and leave Ashley like that though. She's a real sweet kid."

"Yeah, doesn't figure, does it? Not what you or I would do is it? I mean if we were in the same situation."

"No, but then what do you figure the odds would be that we've ever been in the same situation? I mean, *I* was no good at science and *you*..." Frank's voice trailed off as his mouth widened into a grin.

"I was *what*?" Lester demanded, glaring at Frank.

In an uncharacteristically tactful moment, Frank explained, "I didn't know you back then, so...I don't know."

Just then, a boy on a bike darted across the street in front of Lester. "Look out!" Frank cautioned. For the second time in less than a week, Lester narrowly missed running down a boy on a bike, the *same* boy.

Chapter 17

By dusk, Frank and Lester had their evening's provisions loaded onto the pontoon and were ready to shove off. If the old adage, *"Red sky at night-sailors delight"* held any truth, they should have had a magnificent voyage. The setting sun was turning the few clouds in the sky into vivid oranges and crimsons. "Would you look at that," Frank commented, pointing westward.

"Would *you* look at what you're *doing*!" Lester yelled over the egg-beater-like rattle of the motor. "You still need to untie the last rope!"

Frank moved to the rope, mumbling about Lester's general lack of appreciation of his assistance. Once freed from the ties that bound the well-seasoned vessel to its home berth, the two set out on their mission of mischief, unsure of the outcome and totally clueless as to what they were about to experience. Their mission was not only foolish, but totally pointless, given their advanced age. And if their wives ever found out, they would kill them. Thus, it perfectly met all three of the criteria of a grand, high adventure. The anticipation had both men on the verge of giddiness.

No sooner had they cleared the cove that held Lester's dock than they spotted what was surely Ranger Moore's boat at the far end of the lake. Though it appeared motionless, its blue lights were flashing, a sure sign that he was stopping boaters and doing checks of the required nighttime gear. "Just wonderful" muttered Lester. "OK...go check the front lights and I'll check the rest."

"Aye aye, Captain," Frank replied saluting in mockery. From the front platform he shouted, "We're good up here!" He returned to his seat and then turned to ask, "Why so worried, I thought you fixed all those lights today?"

"I *did*, but I wasn't planning on announcing our approach to the beach by having them on. I want to cut the lights and drift by to catch the skinny-dippers off guard. If Dalton's out on the lake, he's likely to notice, that's all."

"Oh!" Frank affirmed his understanding after the usual delay for processing. "Well, while we wait for darkness do you want to try to hook Ol' Wally?"

"You go ahead, I got my hands full just driving and watching for debris."

"Good point. I'll help ya with my spotlight."

As the sun dipped below the western horizon, Legion Lake was finally cloaked in darkness, save the faint light from the full moon. For the next several minutes, the two senior citizens navigated the craft across the lake in the general direction of the beach. Once he saw the float line that surrounded the beach, Lester cut the motor and the lights and dropped the anchors. "Shhh, listen. What do you hear?" Only the sounds of small waves lapping at the pontoon logs answered. Occasionally they could hear laughter coming from one of the cabin decks on the nearby shore, but only a disappointing silence greeted them from the direction of the abandoned beach. As much due to boredom as hunger, Lester opened the plastic bag of Shirley's homemade cookies and took one out. "Cookie?" he asked offering the bag to Frank who took one for precisely the same reason. With the exception of Dalton's boat, Lester's pontoon appeared to be the only craft on the lake.

The two codgers sat quietly listening and watching for any sign of life on shore, but they saw nothing and the only sounds they heard were the barred owls "who-cooks-for-you" or the occasional raucous call of a heron. After nearly 30 minutes of waiting, Lester's patience was nearly gone. "Well, we could be here all...wait...is that a car? Is it coming to the beach?" The two men watched hopefully as a set of headlights moved slowly down the road that led to the beach parking lot and suddenly changed from high beam to parking lamps. As they listened they heard the unmistakable crunch of tires on gravel as the car entered the parking lot and stopped. Once the lights disappeared into the darkness, the outline of the car could be made out.

"What are they doing?" demanded Frank.

"How should I know? Either they're working up their nerve or maybe they're stripping down to their birthday suits. Just be patient." Lester craned his neck in the opposite direction to check on the whereabouts of Ranger Moore's boat. He couldn't be sure, but it seemed like it had not moved.

"Hey, they're getting out," Frank whispered.

First one, and then a second figure, emerged from the car. They picked their way across the grass to the sand at such a slow pace, it was obvious that they were bare-footed. Upon reaching the water, they each dropped something on the sand, let out muffled shrieks, and dashed into the water.

"Aren't you gonna hit the light?"

"Not yet, let them have some fun first," he whispered. "Pass me a beer, why don't ya?" He made one more sweep of the horizon, checking on the ranger's boat before he settled back in the captain's seat and waited for the beer. Although the swimmers held their conversation to a minimum, the laughter they produced confirmed the presence of two females.

"Look, here comes some more!" Frank noted.

But, unlike the first car, this one didn't stop at the parking lot, but continued, headlights blazing all the way across the grass right up to the edge of the sand illuminating the water and revealing not only the two heads bobbing in it, but Lester's pontoon as well. As if the plan hadn't sufficiently turned to crap, a voice from the vehicle's loudspeaker demanded, "Come out of the water, the beach is closed! It's clearly posted, no swimming after 10:00 P.M."

"We can't."

"And why would that be?"

A long silence was the only answer.

"You need to come out of the water immediately, or I will be forced to arrest you."

"We can't, because...we don't have anything on."

Ranger Dalton Moore paused an equally long time. "OK, suit yourselves, but I feel I should tell you, the sheriff's been fishing a dead body out of the water this evening. A *very* dead body."

The scene that unfolded at that point – although far from pretty – will surely be retold in the gossip of the Legion Lake Bait Shop and Coffee Spot for many years to come. Both women screamed at the top of their lungs and immediately stood up in knee deep water and waded toward their towels on shore. Ranger Moore, always the good public servant and gentleman, doused his headlights to afford the women their privacy. Frank, whose impulse control had slumped to an all-time low, switched on his spotlight and lit up the water as brightly as any operating room. Lester, realizing they were now completely busted, decided his only salvation from a ticket and fine from Dalton was to make the craft appear water worthy and switched on the lights revealing the pontoon's outline. This in turn caused Dalton to turn his headlights back on which lead to the women screaming even more loudly and turning away from the shore toward Frank and Lester's position aboard the old pontoon.

"Gloria?"

"Frank?"

"*Shirley?*"

"*Lester!!!*"

"I'm gonna kill pimple-faced Ron!"

Chapter 18

Although the thermometer read 82 degrees as the sun came over the horizon the next morning, there was a definite chill inside the Pierce cabin. Lester stretched in an attempt to remove the kinks from his back and shoulders, but to no avail. The couch he had spent the night on had done quite a number on his arthritic joints. From his vantage point on the couch, he could see that the door to their bedroom was still shut. As he mentally reviewed scenarios for making up with Shirley, he eventually chose the time-honored strategy known as 'skillful neglect.' The decades he had spent getting on and then back off of Shirley's bad side had taught him valuable lessons, number one of which was that he was far better off to wait until she cooled off before approaching her to confess just how stupid he had been during his most recent transgression or how sorry he was afterward. And besides, unlike most of his 'doghouse' situations, this time he wasn't the only one in the wrong. She had some explaining to do herself.

He reviewed the events of the previous evening, mentally preparing his defense in a manner that would have put the average jailhouse lawyer to shame. He mulled over every aspect of the crimes, both his and hers. As he was replaying the sequence for the third time, slumber beckoned. For some reason he became stuck on the sound of Gloria's car tires on the gravel of the beach parking lot, but a new sound – that of someone banging loudly on a door – jolted him to full wakefulness. He realized that someone was indeed knocking but not on their cabin. He pulled himself up into a sitting position and slowly stood on his two aching legs. By the time he reached the window, the banging had been replaced by voices and he could see that they belonged to a scantily clad Ashley and a man on her porch. As his eyes adjusted to the bright sunlight he could see that the car in the driveway was a sheriff's department cruiser and that the man on the porch wore the distinctive hat of a deputy.

He slid the window open just in time to hear the deputy say, "So, I really need you to come with me, miss. I'll wait here for you to get dressed." As a visibly distraught Ashley returned to the cabin, Lester heard the familiar sound of the bedroom door opening inside his own residence. Shirley emerged looking as though she had also spent the night on a couch. "What's going on?" she demanded without making eye contact with Lester.

"I'm not sure. I think Ashley's in some sort of trouble."

Turning back toward the bedroom, "I'd better go over there and help her," she said.

"I don't think you can. The deputy's taking her away."

"Why?"

"I already said, I don't know. I didn't hear that."

They both watched the porch of Ashley's cabin, from separate windows...in silence. A silence which only grew more deafening with each passing minute. Finally, Ashley emerged clothed for the day in an outfit which covered slightly *less* of her personage than the sleep ware from which she had just changed. The deputy held on to her forearm and helped her off the porch and into the backseat of the cruiser. From their vantage point, it was impossible to tell whether he was trying to show emotional support or making sure that she did not flee. Seconds later, the cruiser backed out of the drive and headed down the road.

The departure of the cruiser left the two of them alone with the elephant in the room. Lester decided to launch a trial balloon. "Good morning."

If his effort had any effect, it wasn't apparent. Shirley came away from the window and opened the cupboard for a coffee mug. She filled it with coffee and leaned against the kitchen counter, making eye contact for the first time, but without acknowledging Lester's greeting. Lester desperately wanted a cup of coffee himself, but decided for safety's sake, it could wait until Shirley moved further away from the coffee maker. He took his usual place at the table, waiting for her to make the next move. Another long silence ensued.

Still leaning against the counter, Shirley finally spoke. "I'm mad at you, Lester Pierce!"

Lester wanted to respond with, "Really, I hadn't noticed" but thought better of it. "I know," was his only reply. Another silence followed, but before it ended, Shirley took her place at the table.

"So fishing isn't enough to keep you two entertained. We can't leave you alone for an evening without worrying that you'll become peeping Toms?"

"Peeping Toms? What about you two taking up stripping?"

"Oh please! Nobody would have seen us if you and Frank hadn't been planning your own private peep show."

"Nobody but Dalton."

Another silence afforded Lester a chance to retrieve his own cup of java and return to the table.

"How were we supposed to know he'd decide to come by? He never did before."

"Before? You mean you've done this before?"

For the first time, a slight smile broke from Shirley's pursed lips; one belying pride rather than a sense of humor. "We've been doing it for years. It's been our secret thing. You didn't think we actually drove all the way to Iowa City just to watch a chick flick, did you?"

"Years? And I'm just now finding out about it? Who else knows about this?"

"Nobody, until now! That's what 'a secret' *means*!"

They each took a sip of their coffee, before resuming round two of the argument.

"So what possessed you and Frank to be out on the lake in the dark anyway?"

Changing abruptly to a more sheepish tone he explained "We got a tip...ah that some girls were going to be skinny..."

"So you and Frank *planned* it, thinking you could catch a glimpse of some young skin at the beach?"

Given Shirley's summation, Lester suddenly felt the need to deflect, but the best he could manage was, "It was all Frank's idea." He took another sip of coffee.

"And for your efforts, all you got was a ten-second glimpse of your own wives' behinds?" Shirley's smile morphed into a full out laugh.

On that thought, Lester suddenly coughed and spit coffee across the table. Holding one finger in the air until he could speak again, he added, "Don't forget about the ticket and the fine." And that comment unleashed a coughing jag in Shirley to match.

When they could both speak once again, it became apparent that the worst of the storm had passed and that the Pierces could now move on perhaps putting the "Great Skinny Dipping Fiasco" behind them...as soon as they were through laughing about it. Ever on the watch for a way to turn lead into gold, Lester even thought of suggesting the wives invite the husbands along next time. It was a thought he kept to himself, however.

"Are you ready for some breakfast?"

"Always."

"How do you feel about pancakes?"

"Great!"

"OK then, you make pancakes while I take a nice, *long*, hot shower and try to get all these kinks out of my neck and back," Shirley directed leaving Lester to ponder just how he came to draw both KP duty *and* a cold shower.

Before long, his mind turned to a more important question. *What about the dead body?* He wondered. There had been several drownings at the lake over the years. But Dalton had been very specific in saying 'very dead' and if a very dead drowning victim had been recovered they would have surely heard about an accident or someone being missing long before a 'very dead' body was recovered. No, this didn't seem like a simple case of drowning. It looked like something more sinister.

He retrieved the griddle from under the stove and placed it on a burner igniting a low flame to start the pre-heating process. He then retrieved a can of beer from the fridge and the store brand complete pancake mix from the cupboard, combining just enough mix with the twelve ounces of beer to make a slurry of batter. By the time Shirley was out of the shower and dressed, the batter had risen enough to produce his signature light and fluffy pancakes. He had just removed the last cake from the griddle and was headed for the table with the plate of cakes when they both heard a car pull into the driveway...Ashley's driveway.

Neither of them could resist moving to the window to investigate. It was another sheriff's department car, but this time the Sheriff himself was behind the wheel. And Ashley was in the front seat beside him.

Since they remained in the car, windows up, AC on, it was impossible to hear what they were talking about, but Ashley was clearly upset. Lester wrapped his arm around Shirley as she laid her head on his shoulder and wept. The mystery of the 'very dead' body was much less of a mystery now.

Chapter 19

As soon as the Sheriff exited the cruiser, the Pierces moved into action. After drying her own eyes, Shirley swooped in and helped Ashley into her cabin. Lester began pumping the Sheriff for all the information he could or would give. "All I can tell you at this point is that we pulled the body of a male victim from the lake last night. It appears that the victim had been dead several days. We'll know more after the autopsy. At this point, we're talking to family members of known missing persons in the area and gathering dental records."

"So Ashley...she hasn't been told that it's Brock?"

"Oh no, not at this time. We took her to try to identify some of the clothing, but she couldn't make a positive ID. It's possible no one can, it was in such bad shape."

"You mean because of being in the water for so long?"

"No, that's just it. Neither the body nor the clothing on it appeared to have spent much time in the water." He opened the cruiser door and turned back to Lester. "That's all I'm comfortable saying at this time. Are you folks related to the young lady?"

"No, just neighbors. We're just getting to know her, actually."

"I understand that neither she nor her boyfriend has any family close by. Keep an eye on her and help her, she's probably gonna need it." With that, he shut the door and backed into the street, heading in the direction of town.

Lester stood in the driveway gazing at the surface of the lake and tried to absorb what he had just learned. The glassy smooth surface of the water made the lake appear to be one gigantic mirror reflecting the cloudless sky and the opposing shoreline. A reflection that, for the moment, hid the rocks, tree branches and other debris that lay below the surface. He thought of the countless times over the years that he and Frank had lost lures snagged hopelessly on the lake's bottom as they fished its coves. It certainly wasn't hard to believe that the lake could hold a body for days, even weeks, but how had this body been in the lake long enough to be "long dead" without being in water? Surely he must have been dumped in the lake many days after he died.

He glanced at the door to Ashley's cabin, but there was no sign of Shirley yet; he knew she was doing everything she could to support Ashley and calm her down. He felt certain his presence would not help the situation. He thought of the horror she must have felt trying to identify the clothing. Whether it turned out to be Brock or not having to look at the clothing had undoubtedly unleashed a torrent of horrific thoughts anyone would have a hell of a time getting out of their mind. The poor kid didn't deserve this. No one did. He found himself wanting to do something, anything, to help bring about closure for her. But he had no idea how to help.

Lester was surprised to find himself thinking of her in that way. She had become more than Brock's girlfriend or the blond next door. Something had changed. He had been furious with Brock for running off and leaving him and the others in the lurch in their fight with Wickham. He realized now that he'd also been angry that he'd broken Ashley's heart. And Lester was certain that he'd miss having the kid around, just as a friend. No, something had definitely happened to him; the tears he was wiping away were the proof of that.

He glanced at the breakfast table that held two half empty coffee mugs, two sets of unused plates and silverware and one platter of cold, rubbery pancakes. He decided that Shirley probably wouldn't be much interested in them whenever she returned and that he really had very little appetite as well. He dumped the pancakes in the trash and slid the plate into the sink. Lester had never been the patient type and waiting was certainly not anything he enjoyed. He desperately wanted to know more about the dead body, about the investigation...about Brock. After leaving Shirley a quick note, he headed out for the only place at Legion Lake where any real news was ever to be had.

When he arrived at the Bait Shop and Coffee Spot, he was certain he'd made the right decision as the parking lot was nearly full. That many people never turned out just to drink coffee or eat Ruthie's rolls; they were there to swap what they thought they knew about the latest excitement at the lake with others who probably held even less knowledge. Before he even got up to the door, he could hear the buzz of conversation inside. It occurred to him that, in addition to gossiping about the body, they might also be discussing his and Frank's role in the "Great Skinny-Dipping Caper" but he was willing to risk it. Once inside however, the conversation dropped to whispers even before his eyes adjusted and any doubt about the topic of the gossip was removed. Tucker, the feckless jack-of-all-trades to the lake community fired the first shot. "Well, if it isn't Mr. Peepers? You and Frank have fun last night spying on your wives?" Like everyone else, Tucker had been born ignorant, but he had worked particularly hard to maintain his stupidity all his life and he was proud of his success. A few nervous laughs saluted Tucker's attempt at humor.

"Well, the only reason we were out there was that we'd heard your wife was gonna be one of them!" Lester fired back. Those gathered held nothing back in acknowledging that Tucker had been put in his place.

"What can I get you, Lester?" Ruthie asked.

"Coffee's all. And news if you got any."

"You know me, Lester, I don't gossip. I just provide the fuel for those that do," Ruthie answered as she handed Lester a large, white, ceramic mug full of her best coffee.

"It's not gossip I'm looking for."

Ruthie could tell by his tone that he was on an earnest quest for truth. "I assume you're referring to the drowned man?"

"I am."

"Well, I don't really have much to tell you, except what the deputy who came in for breakfast let slip."

"What was that?"

Ruthie checked to see if any of the gossip mongers had tuned in to their conversation and then leaned in close to Lester. "He said the body was badly scarred up, like maybe he'd been dragged or beaten. I asked him what he thought that meant and he clammed up like he'd given away a state secret or something."

"Did he say anything else? About who they thought it was?"

"No, that's just it; not another word. He threw down a ten-dollar bill and left ASAP. It didn't make any sense."

Lester agreed that neither the food nor the service was worth anywhere near $10, but assumed that she was probably referring to his rapid departure. "He didn't say anything else?"

"Nope, just took off like a rocket."

"How about Dalton? Has he been in?"

"No, and he usually stops in by this time for coffee. Actually, I haven't seen him go by on rounds even. I suppose he's been helping the sheriff, you know paperwork, that sort of crap."

Lester finished his coffee and handed the mug back to Ruthie at the counter. "Well, let me know if you hear anything, will ya?"

"You know it."

As he turned to go, Ruthie announced, "Wait, I just remembered something important. I heard Old Lady Hansen say she intends to sunbathe in the nude this afternoon, you know if you and Frank are interested." Lester shook his head slowly and sighed as he pushed open the door and the room burst into thunderous hoots and howls. "Sorry...You know we all love ya, but I couldn't resist," Ruthie called after him.

Lester knew that what he and Frank had done was immature and stupid. In spite of that, he might have seen fit to try to salvage his honor except that he really couldn't think of a fitting response to Ruthie, and he could feel the vibration of his cell phone in his pocket. Certain it was Shirley telling him it was safe to return home, he answered it without looking at the number. "Yeah, what's up Buttercup?"

After a brief pause, the voice on the other end replied, "This is Dorothy Hickman, Recorder. You asked me to call you about some permits?"

"Oh, yeah, sorry. I thought you were my wife. What did you find?"

"Well, DNR permits for CAFOs in this county do come through this office, but I have nothing from Mr. Wickham. And I'd have been surprised if I did since Lee Wickham is a land investor, not a farmer. He's a frequent user of our office and records, but for his real estate business."

"Yeah, I know about Wickham. Really, nothing? Hasn't he even started the process?"

"Well, he may have the forms from the DNR; he could get those online without our knowledge. All I can tell you is that he hasn't filed anything related to a CAFO in this office."

Lester held the phone to his chest long enough to process what he had learned and issue a heartfelt, "Damn it!" Returning the phone to his ear he asked, "Could he have filed the permits somewhere else?"

"He might have sent them directly to the DNR, but if he did they would have forwarded them to this office, since the permitting process always starts at the county level."

"OK...well thanks for getting back to me. I really appreciate it."

"I don't know if you'd be interested in the rest of what I found or not, but I remembered that Lee Wickham was in here about a month back and tried to drop off an application for a liquor license for another entity, so I looked it up. It was in the name of Aspen Investments."

"Well, thanks for the extra effort, but I don't think that's likely to be related to his CAFO plans, unless he intends to raise pickled pigs feet." Unlike her counterpart in the Treasurers' office, Ms. Hickman possessed a healthy sense of humor as attested by a series of snorts and giggles.

"No, I doubt that. But the reason this stuck in my memory was that liquor licenses are issued to an *owner* of a bar or restaurant for a particular address of operation. He insisted that it wasn't for him, but that he was just dropping it off for a friend. I told him I'd have to have the friend's name, not just the name of the corporation, but he wanted to leave that blank until the application had been approved. When I told him that wouldn't fly, he became very upset with me, and left in a huff."

"OK, but I still don't see..."

"I thought you'd want to know that the address he gave is on the south shore of Legion Lake. In the 4900 block of Shoreline Drive."

"What the hell?"

"I guess I'll have to leave that to *you* to determine. If you need anything else, don't hesitate to ask."

"Thank you very much," Lester tried to add, but she had already hung up.

What the hell, indeed, was Wickham up to?

Chapter 20

"How's she doing?" Lester inquired when Shirley returned.

"Not good, which is to say, I guess, okay. She is scared and she hurts but keeping that inside is never a good thing, and she is certainly not doing that. She keeps trying to find some way to make it not Brock, but the denial won't last."

"What do you think?"

"About the body?" Shirley clarified. "I'm sure the sheriff is trying to be thorough and there are probably other explanations, but right now...I'd really hate to be Ashley."

Lester nodded his agreement. "What can we do?"

"I think the best thing we can do is to keep an eye on her and just let be as it plays out. It will take a bit before her life gets anywhere near normal... and that is probably the same for us," Shirley said wryly.

After spending the entire summer so far trying to protect the Legion Lake community and finding out that the only man who had offered any real help was either missing or dead, Lester wondered what "normal" would look like. Maybe the plaque on their cabin wall was right-maybe normal was "just a setting on the washing machine."

"Whether it's Brock or not, I'm really concerned. Someone died out on our lake and it doesn't sound like an accident."

"We don't know that for sure. It might have been an accident, and he might have died elsewhere and been dumped here."

"And that would be so much better...why? No, I'll feel a lot better when we all know what happened and to whom. Until then, I think we at least need to lock the doors, and it wouldn't hurt for you to find the shells for your old gun,"

"You mean the *old* shells that probably won't even fire? So one of us can blow the other one away in the dark when we are coming back from the bathroom? No thanks! That gun has been collecting dust above the fireplace for 30 years for a reason and I'm not about to put it into service now!"

"You mean you're *not* worried?" asked Shirley

"If I thought there was some lunatic running around out here killing people, I'd be a lot more likely to want to just go back home until he was caught. But I don't think that."

Shirley took a long sigh and looked at her husband of nearly 50 years. "Well, what do you think is going on?"

"I think they pulled a body out of the lake and they will let us know what happened as soon as they get all the facts and figure it out. That's what I think. Until then, we'll just have to wait and see. It's not like it is on TV – they can't solve this in 60 minutes. Until the sheriff gets it figured out we just need to be on the watch for things out of the ordinary. We should keep our eyes open and anything that seems unusual, we ought to tell him."

Shirley moved in close to put her arm around Lester and laid her head on his shoulder. "You're probably right. I'm sorry I lost it. I guess I'm just worried. What you said makes a lot of sense."

Lester was pleased that she had at least left the door open to the possibility that he had said something sensible for a change. He thought his speech would have made a lot more sense if he had believed a word of it himself. A change of subject seemed like a good idea. "Hey, what have you heard from Gloria lately? How're Frank's treatments coming? He never says anything about the cancer and I'm kind of afraid to bring it up."

"She's the same way, but I think she'd come to me if things weren't going well. We should have them over for dinner. Maybe tonight after it cools off some we could sit out on the deck and have some burgers, maybe a little wine, like we used to do?"

"You make a list of food we need and I'll go clean off the grill and sweep the deck."

"The deck could use a little sprucing up, so go ahead. I'll call them to see if they can even come tonight."

An hour later the Pierces were on their way into town for groceries, wine and beer. And since neither of them had had any breakfast, Lester sprung for an early lunch. Before 3:00, they had everything in place, ready for their guests. "Want some tea?" Shirley asked pouring herself a tall glass. "I'm going to sit in the shade and read until it's time to get ready."

"Sounds good, but I'll get it. You go ahead, I'll be right out." Lester opened the slider for her and she headed for her favorite spot under the maple tree, glass in one hand and her current novel in the other. Lester followed soon after toting his own glass of tea and a stack of woodworking magazines to the hammock. Moments later Shirley was well into her book and Lester had nodded off, open magazine face down over his chest. And so the afternoon passed, much as afternoons at the lake had always passed before Wickham or Brock or Ashley had become such a large part their of lake life. And though neither had considered it, this uneventful afternoon was evidence that their life at Legion Lake had returned at least to the welcome pace of the past.

By 5 o'clock, the shade the maple had provided so generously earlier in the afternoon had moved much further east, covering the deck area like a gigantic blanket. Shirley prodded Lester awake, telling him to light the grill. He eventually roused his arthritic bones from the hammock and started the fire in the grill, before heading inside for a quick shower and a change of clothes. Promptly at a quarter past six, Frank's one-eyed truck pulled into the Pierce driveway. Lester took it as a good sign that Frank had driven, but his optimism was dampened a bit by the fact that he began hacking and coughing as soon as he stepped out of the truck and started the walk up the drive.

"Hey, welcome. What can I get you to drink?"

"Cold beer if you got it, a warm one if you don't," Frank chuckled.

"How about you, Gloria?"

"A diet cola would be great."

Lester fished around in the ice chest for the drinks and passed them to the Mariboes helping himself to a beer in the process.

"So what have you two been up to?"

"Just the usual," Gloria answered. "I've been taking a lot of pictures and then...of course...Frank's treatments," she added quickly taking a sip of diet cola.

"How's that going Frank?" Shirley asked.

"Oh, OK, I guess. I don't get much out of the doctor. He looks at the tests and then tells me I need to keep coming back. You know what they say, 'No news is good news', right?"

Lester and Shirley each expressed their agreement, although neither was convinced. Shirley excused herself and entered the cabin to retrieve the burgers for the grill.

"How's it going with the fight against Wickham's CAFO?" Frank asked.

"Oh, I almost forgot. I have some *news*...I heard from the County Recorder about Wickham's permits. He hasn't done a thing!"

"Well I'll be...what does that mean do ya think?"

"I have no idea, but that's not all. He *has* applied for a liquor license for someone else out here on the south shore of the lake."

"What the heck would he do with a liquor license out here?"

"I don't know, but he applied for it under the name of some corporation called Aspen Properties."

At that point, Shirley exited the cabin carrying a tray of burger patties and asked, "Who, Les?"

"Wickham, who else?"

Setting the tray down on the shelf of the grill, Shirley replied sternly, "We're not going to talk about Wickham or anything else unpleasant! Tonight is about having fun like we used to before all this...this *crap* came up, OK?"

From that point on the subject changed and the four long-time friends reminisced about past summers at the lake with Frank and Lester taking turns cracking everyone up. Each brought up stories of the other's antics over the years, some of which were news to the wives. Lester finally brought the house down recalling a moment from one of their fishing misadventures. "It was just like a scene from a movie. We were just getting ready to back away from the dock. Frank was wearing those stupid red suspenders and I sent him to the bow to untie the front rope. When he bent down to reach the rope, his suspender caught on a nail on the dock railing and I didn't know it. He yelled something which I couldn't hear because of the motor, but when I saw him waving his hand, I put it in reverse and gave it the gas. Frank shot off the front platform and into the water. It looked like someone had tried to shoot a bowling ball with a slingshot, except the bowling ball had on red suspenders and was swearing...in Norwegian!"

The resulting hoots from the wives and Lester were too much to resist, even for Frank and he eventually raised his beer as if giving a toast and after a slight pause uttered, "Uff Da!!" which led to another round of laughter and added to the tears running down cheeks.

"That slingshot would have been nice to have last night," Gloria added, causing a momentary pause in the laughter as they looked each other in the eye.

Breaking the silence, Frank asked, "To shoot me *away* from the beach or *toward* it?" which led to another round of laughter and tears running down the cheeks; this time, eye contact was only between spouses.

"Frank, tell them about the time we took the kids to the water park in Texas and you got stuck in the giant tube slide," Gloria insisted.

"No, we don't have to go into that..."

"Come on Frank, don't stop now," Shirley begged.

"There's not much to tell. We were at a water park and Steve dared his old man to go down the big slide, one of those enclosed tube-types made outta the see-through plastic, with several turns and loops in it, and I did, that's all!"

"Yeah and he got *stuck* in one of loops!" Gloria added.

"God man, how'd you get out?" asked Lester.

"Well, the water kept building up behind me until it finally just flushed me out."

"Looked sort of like a giant turd inside a see-through sewer pipe," Gloria explained.

"Good thing too, because they'd already sent the maintenance man to get the giant plunger," Frank added to everyone's delight.

"And if that hadn't worked, they would have had no choice but to pour in 50 gallons of Liquid Plumber®, right Frank?"

When she could speak again, Shirley observed, "I swear, the older you get, the more dangerous it is to let you two old coots be alone together!" She then pointed out the time and suggested Lester turn the burgers on the grill. There was general agreement among the guests to both of her points. As she watched the two men move toward the grill,

Shirley commented to Gloria, "It's nice to see that Frank is claiming his Norwegian heritage again. I assume he's forgotten about being a Jew?"

"You'd think. We still go to the Lutheran church on Sundays and he still likes his lutefisk, but he just ordered another yarmulke on the internet and says he plans to wear it on Saturdays. What that young man told him about his ancestors has really taken hold of him and I haven't been able to convince him that it doesn't matter, that he's still Norwegian, cause that's how he was raised. Sort of like lutefisk by any other name..."

"Still smells?"

"Yeah, uff da, to that!"

As they both laughed at Gloria's little joke, Shirley felt some hope that life would indeed get back to normal. But as two sheriffs' cruisers approached on the road leading into the park, normal was about to take an ugly turn. All four friends turned and watched in silence as the cars slowed, signaled for a turn and pulled into the gravel driveway leading up to Ashley's cabin. As they watched, the Sheriff and a female deputy exited their cruisers and walked slowly up the drive toward the door. They waited breathlessly for Ashley to answer the knock on the door, afraid to even speak, until Gloria broke the silence whispering, "That name 'Aspen'...I'm pretty sure that was Miriam Wickham's maiden name!"

Chapter 21

The four friends didn't have long to wait to have their common fear confirmed. As soon as Ashley opened the door, they heard a very solemn Sheriff ask, "Ashley, may we come in? I'm afraid we have some bad news."

Although none of them wanted to believe what they were hearing, each of them expressed their acceptance of what the sheriff's visit meant – the body found in the lake was Brock Sanford. Frank was the first to sit down, followed by his wife who immediately sought and found his hand. Lester put his arm around Shirley and pulled her tight to his side. Both women wept openly as their men shed tears in silence.

After a torturously long wait of minutes, the sheriff emerged from the cabin and walked briskly toward the couples waiting on the deck. From his position on the lawn next to the deck, he asked to speak to Mr. Pierce. Lester, taking command of the situation, replied only, "You can call me Lester. Come on up here."

"The dental records of Brock Sanford match the body we found yesterday in the lake, and, although we haven't yet determined the cause of death, we haven't ruled out foul play. Because we haven't been able to locate or even determine his next of kin, I thought I should inform Miss Edwards...uh, Ashley. My deputy is with her now and will try to obtain further information from her about next of kin as it seems appropriate."

Shirley stepped toward the sheriff and asked, "How is she holding up?"

"I'm afraid she took it pretty hard, as you can imagine. My deputy will stay with her for awhile, but if you feel you could give her support, you might want to offer..."

"I can go over right now," Shirley offered.

"Me too!" Gloria added.

"I'd wait a few minutes and let Deputy Meyers be alone with her. She's very skilled at these things, but she'll no doubt be called away sooner or later. We never have enough personnel, it seems."

At that point, the sheriff's radio blurted out something decipherable only to him and he said simply, "You'll have to excuse me, but I have to go. I asked Deputy Meyers to stop over before she leaves." And, with that, he entered his cruiser and drove down the road, exiting the park, lights flashing.

The four friends had a collective sigh eventually turning and looking at each other. "I somehow thought it was Brock," Shirley confessed. "I hoped it wasn't, but I think I knew it only made sense."

"Poor Ashley. I wonder what she'll do. I don't think she even has a job. Brock was probably paying the bills," Gloria wondered.

"How much you want to bet, Wickham had something to do with this?" Lester asked.

"Lester! Don't even say that! I know he's a class-A slime ball, but I can't believe he is a murderer," Shirley admonished. Then, her brow furrowed, she turned to Gloria and asked, "Wait, what were you saying about his wife?"

"That name Aspen...I was saying that was Miriam's name before she married Wickham. I remember she mentioned that once."

"So that's why the property is in the name of Aspen Investments...It's just a shell corporation he planned to hide behind so he could carry out whatever crooked plan he's up to and we wouldn't find out it was him. That money-grubbing bastard!"

Realizing Frank hadn't spoken a word or moved out of his tracks since the sheriff left, Gloria asked, "Frank, are you OK?"

"I can't believe it. I was just beginning to like the kid. And now he's gone." With that, he turned to face the lake, pulled his shirt tail out of the waist of his shorts where it had been neatly tucked and deliberately tore the shirt tail.

"Frank! What are you doing?" Shirley demanded.

"It's OK...it's a Jewish thing," Gloria explained.

Wanting more information, but sensing a fuller explanation could wait for a better time, Shirley replied, "Oh."

"Excuse me," a voice from Ashley's yard said. "I'm deputy Meyers. I believe the sheriff explained what has happened here?" Nods from all four affirmed her assumption. "I've been talking with Ashley, consoling her and trying to find out what I could about next of kin. I understand Ashley and Brock weren't married?"

"No, just living together."

"Well, she says he had no close relatives, that he was raised by an uncle in Illinois, whom she believes to be in a rest home. Can you confirm any of that?"

The four friends shared blank looks in answer to her question.

"She says Mr. Sanders was a student at Iowa. We'll reach out to the registrar in the morning and see if he listed any emergency contacts, but it looks like Ashley may be it. I called her mother for her, but I didn't get the feeling that she would be the source of much comfort. Anyway, Ashley speaks highly of Mrs. Pierce. If you can keep an eye on her and support her, I think that she'd welcome your help. She's having a very hard time right now."

"Do you have any idea what happened?" Shirley asked.

"I can't speculate on that. The body is at the DCI lab in Ankeny for an autopsy. When their report comes back, we should have a cause of death, until then we will continue to investigate and gather information. Just know that we won't give up until we solve this. As with all cases, time is both our friend and our enemy. If you can help her, that would be the best thing you could do for now. I'm sorry, but I need to get back to my other duties. If you think of anything that could help us, please get in touch with me." With that, Deputy Meyers handed each of them her card then entered her cruiser and drove out of the park.

"I still say he was murdered," Lester insisted. "The sheriff said he was badly beaten up; he didn't get that way falling out of his kayak!"

"Well, we'll find out soon enough. Right now that poor girl needs help. On top of everything else, she'll probably have a burial to plan and pay for if there aren't any relatives."

Lester felt a rising anger within himself unlike anything he could remember before. A young man was dead, his girlfriend was heartbroken and something very peculiar was happening with property just down the road from his own. Every instinct he had told him Wickham was behind all of it. And he knew he wouldn't have a moment's peace the rest of the summer until his suspicions were addressed.

Chapter 22

"Did Ashley say whether Brock's uncle was coming?" asked Lester.

"Oh no, he can't make the trip, he's too old and frail. She thought he was sending flowers and she intends to send him a copy of the video."

"Oh, that'll be nice," Lester answered, thinking it would be anything but, since the poor guy had only one relative and even he wouldn't be there. "At least it should be a nice day. Look at that sky." Lester knew from all his years living in Iowa that a cloudless sky in the morning wasn't a rock solid guarantee of good weather all day, but it was usually a good sign. And the weather man wasn't predicting anything but sunshine and temperatures in the 80s. At least Brock would get a good sendoff.

He had to hand it to Ashley, she had spunk. Somehow she had pulled together enough energy to organize what promised to be a respectful service. The donation jar at the Coffee Spot had brought in enough money for cremation and she had asked Lester to take her out to the center of the lake where she planned to scatter his ashes shortly after the one o'clock ceremony. And much to everyone's surprise, by 12:30 a crowd had actually gathered by the public boat ramp where Lester's freshly scrubbed pontoon was moored. Besides the usual curiosity seekers, Ed Groves had come to pay his respects along with at least a dozen of the construction crew. And a handful of young men and women Brock's age who were likely college friends had gathered. Even Charlie from the ICEP was in attendance.

Promptly at one, a minister from town stepped to the shoreline and addressed the crowd. "Friends, loved ones...we gather today to commit the soul of our comrade Brock Alan Sanford. At 24, he was taken far too early. Even though we have trouble believing this was God's plan, we must accept what has happened. He leaves behind the love of his life, Ashley. I'm sure she takes great comfort in the support she can draw from those in attendance."

Ashley, dressed in black jeans and a dark gray blouse stood between Shirley and Gloria sobbing, holding a very plain metal container of ashes. She nodded her head in agreement. Shirley extended her arm and pulled Ashley to her side. She laid her head on Shirley's shoulder and wept openly. At that point, the minister offered a prayer, but Lester paid little attention – his eyes were fixed on a heartbroken Ashley, his mind on Wickham. As the pastor droned on, Lester cast his gaze away from Ashley and over the crowd.

The crowd started to move, forming an opening to allow Ashley and the minister to approach the balloon-clad pontoon. A nudge from Shirley told Lester that the minister must have indicated it was time to "release the cremated remains" while he was focused elsewhere. He quickly returned to the matter at hand and moved down the ramp dock ahead of the procession to open the side gate of the pontoon. The vessel had been built to hold ten people, but Lester turned away all but the first six since that was the number of life jackets he had. Even though Dalton had agreed to look the other way as they scatted the remains, he was certain he wouldn't ignore any safety violations.

The trek to the middle of the lake took only a few minutes in spite of the respectfully slow speed provided by the over-taxed motor. The plan called for Lester to steer the craft into a large circle in the center of the lake, but again he found his mind drifting. Once away from the public dock, and out onto the lake, his attention was drawn to the opposite shore. He couldn't believe his eyes – sitting right on the end of his own boat dock, like a king holding court, taking the whole thing in with binoculars was *Wickham* himself! Lester felt certain that had there not been half a lake separating them, he would not have been able to refrain from punching him or at least pushing him off his throne and into the water!

Another nudge from Shirley brought Lester back to his captain's duties. He turned the wheel slightly to the left and brought the pontoon into a wide circular trajectory. Ashley opened the box of flower petals and passed it around the boat asking everyone to take a handful for spreading on the water. Frank, yarmulke in place, took the last handful of petals. He also retrieved an item from the pocket of his bright green shirt. As the craft moved in its circular path, the occupants followed Ashley's lead and, one by one, released their flower petals onto the water's surface. Frank released his allotment of petals along with a small toy kayak. At the signal from the minister, Lester cut the motor and bowed his head along with the others. "Before we commit these remains to the water and the soul from which they came into God's care, I have been asked to share a poem in tribute." He stepped to the railing and, in a very few words, managed to summarize pretty much everything Lester and the others knew about Brock and all the unknowns as well.

Not, How Did He Die,
But How Did He Live?

Not how did he die, but how did he live?
Not what did he gain, but what did he give?
These are the units to measure the worth
Of a man as a man, regardless of birth.
Not, what was his church, nor what was his creed?
But had he befriended those really in need?
Was he ever ready, with word of good cheer,
To bring back a smile, to banish a tear?
Not what did the sketch in the newspaper say,
But how many were sorry when he passed away.

If Lester had had any remaining doubts that Brock would have approved of his service, the poem Ashley chose absolutely crushed them.

As Ashley stepped to the railing, everyone else stepped back to the center of the deck, leaving her alone with the minister. She opened the tin and, handing it to the minister to hold, she took one handful of its contents after another and scattered them lovingly onto the surface of the water. Eventually she upended the tin, emptying the last bit into her hand. She closed her fist around its contents, gave it a kiss and cast the last few ashes onto the lake. The silence that followed was broken by Frank who uttered *"Jeg savner deg"* quietly. Motioning to the other four with his right hand, the minister took his left arm off of Ashley's shoulder and untied the string holding one of the brightly colored balloons to the railing. The others followed suit until all 21 balloons were aloft, treating the sky above Legion Lake to a rainbow of colors. While everyone gazed upward to follow the flight of the balloons, no one was watching Ashley. Apparently having exceeded her tolerance for the emotional toll of the service, she began to wobble and then her legs gave out completely. She collapsed with a resounding thud onto the plywood deck of the pontoon. The collective gasp alerted the minister who was just beginning another prayer. He instantly changed course and, in one seamless move, slid his life preserver under her head and produced smelling salts from his shirt pocket. As the shocked passengers waited breathlessly for signs of her revival, they could hear a very faint but heartfelt rendering of "Amazing Grace" coming from the crowd gathered at the shore. The only other sound to be heard was the tearing of a bright green shirt tail.

Chapter 23

The talk at the Coffee Spot the next morning was divided between comments about the beautiful service Ashley had arranged for Brock and speculation as to what had led to a need for same. "People on shore were really touched by the service. And so many asked about Ashley," Frank reported to Lester through the truck window. "I wish you could have been there to hear them. Your name even came up a few times, and they was all good comments. People thought you really stepped up, taking her out on the lake and all."

"Well, that's nice to hear, but I was glad to do it and honored that she asked me. What do *they* think happened?"

"Oh, most of them agree with you that somebody beat him to death. They were pretty clear on that."

"Did anyone's name come up as a suspect?"

"Oh, no. Nobody seemed to have anyone in particular in mind."

"Or, they were just afraid to say what they thought!"

"Yeah, maybe. I don't think anybody else feels the same way about it we do," Frank observed.

"Well, I don't think the sheriff has even scratched the surface of it yet. As far as I know, they haven't even released a cause of death, and they must know or they wouldn't have released the body to Ashley for cremation."

"Yeah, good point."

"You know as well as I do that damned Wickham had something to do with this. Who else had any reason to wish Brock harm?"

"Yeah, I agree with that sure enough. But until the sheriff finds the evidence, what can we do about it?"

"Well, that sheriff doesn't strike me as the Sherlock Holmes type. If we sit around and wait for the evidence to drop in his lap, this thing will never get settled."

"So, what can we do?"

Lester took his time in formulating an answer, casting his eyes out over the waters of the lake and drawing a deep breath. Finally, he punctuated his thoughts with a small tap of his fist on the door of Frank's truck. "I don't know how yet Frank, but we're gonna find out what happened to Brock if it takes the rest of the summer. Somewhere out here there are answers and we're either gonna find them or make sure that sheriff keeps looking until he does!"

"Are you sure that's a good idea, Les? I mean what if we do something wrong and mess up the case against Wickham, you know wind up making it hard to convict him or...give him...what do they call it...grounds for an appeal?"

Lester looked into the eyes of his old friend, shook his head and said simply, "You watch too much *Law and Order*. I'm just saying we need to keep our eyes and ears open for anything that could help the sheriff determine who killed him. Maybe it wasn't Wickham. Maybe there's a serial killer running around beating biology students to death."

Frank's brow furrowed briefly as he considered that possibility.

"I'm kidding Frank. I'm just saying when you hear hoof beats, maybe you should be looking for a horse and not a zebra. There's a car coming, you better head on down the road."

Frank, his confusion further deepened by talk of horses and zebras, put his truck in gear and drove off toward his cabin, hoping Gloria could make some sense of what Lester had just said. Lester on the other hand, knew exactly what to do next. He needed to find more information and thought he knew just the place to look; the 4900 block of Shoreline Drive.

"I'm going for a walk," he yelled through the open kitchen window to Shirley.

"OK, sounds good. I was just about to pay Ashley a visit and see how she's doing."

Lester Pierce had never been a fan of physical activity and, before he had gone 100 yards, he began to wish he had taken the riding mower, or maybe even the truck. As he trudged along, he realized what made him make such a foolish decision – he was pissed! And though he knew he had every reason to be, he also knew if he was going to accomplish anything, he'd have to calm down. As his pace returned to normal, his slow walk began to be a source of enjoyment although he wasn't ready to admit that yet. He began to notice things about his neighbors' properties as he passed them, details that he had never even seen as he sped by in his truck. The Fergusons had an outdoor kitchen. The Russells had an above-ground pool in their back yard. And nearly every house had hostas.

The further he went, the more he realized how little he really knew about the properties and people right in his own area of Shoreline Drive. He had been driving this road for more than three decades but everywhere he looked, cabin after cabin, the scene was repeated. He noticed details about the properties that had escaped his attention on every other trip. As he considered this fact, he forgot about pig farms and Wickham and Brock. And, for a few minutes, Lester Pierce actually enjoyed himself.

Eventually, he had walked far enough from his own place that he couldn't put a name to the owners of all the properties. He had come to a section of Shoreline Drive that definitely was not the pride of the lake, a cluster of a half dozen modest but well-kept homes that had probably been built back in the '40s. Across the street were four cabins that surrounded a dilapidated old dancehall. Long ago closed, the dance hall had once been the center of activity at the lake and nearly everyone who lived there had spent several evenings a summer dancing, drinking or just enjoying the sunset from the large deck that hung out over the shore. Or, so he had heard from the old timers. The doors had already closed before he and Shirley bought property. And now, it sat as a gigantic, sagging eyesore inside a sea of weeds.

As he stood in the road, an old woman came around the corner of the tidy little cottage two doors beyond the dance hall. She stopped to look at Lester, lifted her hand to her brow to block the sun from her eyes and then waved a very friendly hello. Lester waved back out of courtesy without recognizing the woman. At that point, she turned her attentions to the flower bed in front of her cabin. As Lester turned back to the rotting building in front of him, his eye caught a glimpse of something in the weeds. As he moved in for a closer view, he recognized it as one of the steel posts the county had put in front of every property years ago to hold the street number. This one had obviously fallen victim to a mower or more likely a passing snow plow. He pushed aside the weeds and tried to pick up the post but one end was still buried several feet in the ground and the remainder was actually bent level with the surface. This was definitely the work of a snow plow. The house number was still attached, but covered in dried mud. Lester kicked at it with his shoe and uncovered the numbers "4955".

Suddenly, Lester felt his anger returning although he wasn't entirely sure why. Still standing on the edge of the road, he turned around to get a full 360 degree look at the surrounding properties. Everywhere he saw the same thing, nondescript little two bedroom bungalows, most covered in the fake log siding that had been popular long ago. Wondering just what Wickham had seen in this area, his eyes settled on the unit next door to the weed patch. He took a few steps in that direction to get a better look and noticed another of the wooden signs so many of the properties sported to announce the name of the owner. When he was close enough to make out the name, it read "Urlichsons." Since there was no sign of life at the Urlichson house, he made a beeline for the house just beyond where the older woman was still digging in her flower bed.

"Pardon me, miss."

"It's Mrs., Mrs. Evelyn Hansen." A very spry Evelyn Hansen rose to her feet and turned to face him. "Lester Pierce, I presume," she said smiling, removing a muddy glove and extending a hand in his direction.

"Oh, I'm sorry Mrs. Hansen, I didn't recognize you earlier and I guess I've never known where your place was. So what're you up to, planting flowers this late in the summer?"

Frowning briefly, she explained, "No, I'm digging them up. I'm moving into town into that new retirement place. There's a nice little garden spot right by my front door, and I don't see any reason to leave these for the next guy."

"So you *have* sold? You didn't let the talk about the hog farm scare you off did you?"

"Lester, an old widow like me has to look out for herself. I wanted to live the rest of my life out here, but when that came up, I started thinking who was I kidding? I have no business trying to keep this place up. It needs a new roof, the gutters fill up with leaves every fall and, just between you and me, I think the wells going bad. When he approached me about selling I wasn't ready, but after I found out about the pig farm, well that did it. And it didn't hurt that he offered cash!"

"Cash?"

"Yep, got what I was asking, every penny. And more, actually. Already got it in the bank. Come September 1st, I move into town and he gets the keys."

"But he's already paid you? Who pays more than full price in advance...before closing?"

"He did, that's all I cared about. We closed weeks ago, but he agreed to let me live here rent free until I was ready to move this fall."

Lester had to take a few moments to let it all soak in. He studied the cabin covered in stucco and ivy vines. Judging from the outward appearance of the structure, it needed all the repairs Mrs. Hansen had listed and likely thousands of dollars more. He couldn't imagine what Wickham, or anybody else for that matter, would want with the place. Particularly if property values were likely to plummet after the CAFO was built. "Whoa, back up. What did you just say? Did you just say that you didn't decide to sell until *after* you heard about the pig farm?

"Yes, that's right. I was really relieved to find out he was still interested even though he had offered to buy out anybody else after they found out about the pig farm."

"You mean he approached you about buying your place *before* he made the offer to buy any property out here?"

"Oh, heavens yes. He's been after me to sell for over a year. Urlichson's too. But, like I said, I guess I was just fooling myself, thinking that I could continue to keep up with the place."

"Well, I'll be a son of a bitch!"

"I beg your pardon?"

"Mrs. Hansen, I could just kiss you!" No sooner had the words left his lips than he regretted them.

Backing away, a suddenly suspicious Mrs. Hansen turned the point of her garden trowel at him. "Lester, I think it's time for you to leave."

"I'm sorry, Mrs. Hansen, I just mean that...well you have no idea of the importance of what you just told me, that's all. Thank you! Thank you!" And with that, Lester did indeed leave her property. He stepped back onto the lawn of the Urlichson place and made the same quick assessment of that building. What he saw was another structure badly in need of repair, cracks in the foundation, rotted window frames, soffit material hanging loose from the underside of the roof and dozens of missing shingles. He turned and started to walk back in the direction of his own cabin, but after a few paces, he pulled his phone from his back pocket and dialed. "Shirley, I'm down by the old dance hall and I need a ride home."

"You're either going to have to wait or walk back. Ashley and I are having a heart to heart."

"Oh, swell!" Lester uttered as he began his retreat toward home. With the sun nearing its midday apex, he began a walk far less enjoyable than when he had covered the same stretch of Shoreline Drive an hour earlier. As he reached his own driveway, he noticed Shirley exiting Ashley's cabin, carefully closing the screen door to prevent it from slamming. *Perfect timing,* he thought. "I guess I should have waited."

"Shhh," Shirley whispered, holding her finger to her lips as she walked back to their own steps. "She just fell asleep and we need to talk."

"Sleep? It's almost noon!"

"She's been sick. Can't keep anything down. And unless I'm mistaken, its *morning sickness!*"

Seldom at a loss for words, Lester slumped silently onto the bottom step of his deck and simply shook his head.

Chapter 24

"That's right, 4955 Shoreline Drive. The name is Urlichson." Lester waited as the Recorder's assistant searched for the information. "July 15th? Of this year? And who was the buyer?"

"Aspen Properties, but Lee Wickham handled the transaction."

"And the price?"

"Well it appears that they paid $115,500."

"Really? Thank you! Thank you very much? You've been *very* helpful!"

Lester finished jotting down the figure and then flipped through the pages he had printed from the County Assessor's website. "Well, there it is, just like with Mrs. Hansen. Wickham paid Urlichsons right at 25% more than the fair market value for their place. And he hasn't settled with any other property owners out here. He definitely wanted those two properties next to the ruins of the old dance hall. But why? And what does this have to do with Brock's death?"

"Lester, you've got to stop saying that. We don't know that he had anything to do with Brock," Shirley warned.

"Maybe you don't, but I do. I can just feel it."

"And, it sounds like he just made up that whole story about the CAFO to scare them into wanting to sell their properties," Frank observed making a particularly astute connection.

"Absolutely! I tell you he's capable of anything. I don't know how yet, but I know he's the reason Brock Sanford is dead!"

"Well, just keep your voice down. If you're right about him and he gets wind of your talk, who knows, he might come after you or me."

Shirley's cautionary advice brought a somber tone to the weekly gathering at the Beer Garden, a typically lighthearted affair. They all sat silently as they considered her warning. Realizing she was responsible for the sudden chill, Shirley changed the subject. Pointing to the opposite shore, she said, "Look, that sailboat across the lake is raising its sail. I hope it comes this way. I love to watch them glide by. It's so peaceful."

As the others turned to look out over the lake, Shirley continued. "So Gloria, I hear some of your pictures are posted for sale inside. Way to go!"

"Yeah, Ruthie thought they were so good she hung them on the wall by the register until somebody buys them."

"When did she do that?" Lester asked, realizing he had not noticed them.

"Oh, a couple of weeks ago, at least."

Lester couldn't be certain, but guessed he and Frank frequented the Coffee Spot at least every other day. The fact that he had paid for coffee that many times without noticing a change in the motif behind the register – let alone Gloria's photography – was a concern. "I hadn't noticed, Gloria. I suppose this thing with Brock has a hold of me worse than I realized. I'll make a point to look at them when I go in to pay this time."

"That's OK, Lester. We've all been pretty upset about Brock. Had it not been for that, this could have been a perfect summer."

"Yeah, and who knows how many of those we..." Shirley's voice trailed off as she realized how completing her thought would make Gloria feel. Searching for a change of subject she pointed to the road leading down to the dock. "Oh, look at that boy on the bike. Why is he riding standing up? I never had a bike, but I always wondered why boys sometimes do that."

Without looking, Lester answered, "It gives an advantage going up a hill. You can use all your weight to push down on the pedal instead of just your leg muscles."

"Yeah, but he's doing it because the bike's way too big for him," Frank added. "I noticed that when you almost ran over him in town."

"What? Lester almost hit a kid? When?" Shirley demanded.

"Frank, are you sure it's the same kid?" Lester asked, suddenly interested.

"Same blue bike. Same scrawny..."

"Frank, you're gonna have to give Shirley a ride home!" Lester said as he handed Shirley a twenty and headed for his truck.

The kid had enough of a head start that Lester could not catch up to him before he darted down the path toward town. Pounding on the steering wheel in frustration, Lester headed out of the park at a speed that would have caused Dalton to empty his ticket book, but fortunately he was nowhere to be seen. One rolling stop later he was out on the main road into town where he eventually realized that, even if he slowed to the speed limit, he was certain to beat any kid on a bike into town.

Since the path was actually an abandoned rail bed, it was easy enough for Lester to find a spot to "ambush" the kid. He parked his truck across the trail close to where it exited the surrounding timber. The minutes that passed, seemed like hours, as he waited in a vantage point well out of view. He realized he'd risked a ticket for nothing and once again attributed that to his obsession with solving the mystery of Brock's death. He took a few deep breaths and managed to reduce the pounding in his chest. Realizing he had put himself in a perfect position not only to detain the boy but also to appear as either a child molester or an inept kidnapper, he stepped out from his position in the bushes just as the whir of the mountain bike's knobby tires became audible in the distance. Opting for a more straightforward approach, he stood in the middle of the path, cranked his face into his best smile and motioned for the boy to stop – which he did.

"I know you! You're the asshole that tried to run me over a few days ago!" Standing again on the pedals he attempted to speed off but Lester managed a firm grip on the handle bars and held the bike still.

"Yes I am, and I'm very sorry about that. That's why I stopped you. I wanted to apologize."

Looking only slightly relieved, the kid rested on the crossbar and put one foot on the paved surface of the trail.

"You kind of shot out in front of me before I saw you but it would have been on me if you'd been hurt. I'm the adult and I was driving the truck, so it was really my fault. I'm sorry."

As the boy's trepidation dissipated, he relaxed his stance on the bike and almost lost his balance in the process. As Lester steadied the bike with one hand, he held out the other in an offer to shake. The boy accepted, shook Lester's hand and said, "It's OK. I'm sorry I called you an asshole."

"Don't worry about it. I'm afraid I've called a few people that myself. I'm Lester. And you're..."

"Jonah."

"And your last name is...?"

"Bennett."

"Jonah, like in the whale?" Getting no response, he moved on. "That's quite a bike you have there," Lester observed as he moved to inspect the other side. "Must have cost you a fortune."

"Not really. I found it."

"Found it? Where?"

"By the lake. Some rich kid ditched it and I found it buried under some brush. Now it's mine!"

"Why do you think another kid ditched it?"

"Cause that's what they do. Kids at my school do it all the time. They get tired of their bikes so they ditch them and tell their folks they were stolen, so they'll buy them a new one."

"Ditch them out by the lake, do they?"

"No, usually in the creek by the school." The look on Jonah's face told Lester that reality was beginning to sink in.

"Too bad it's so big for you. What makes you so sure it was a kid's bike?"

Jonah's brow furrowed as he considered all that Lester had brought to his attention. "I gotta go, mister."

"Lester, remember? You know my friend, a grown man, lost a bike just like this one. Out at the lake."

"I gotta go. Let go of my bike. I gotta get home."

"His bike had a big dent in the underside of the frame, and I'll bet if we turn this bike over it will have one too."

"No, it's *my* bike. I found it! Now let go of it!"

"Jonah, calm down. I'll make you a deal. If this is my friend's bike, I'm sure there'll be a reward. And if that's not enough to buy you a bike that actually fits you, I'll make up the difference. How about it? Do we have a deal?"

Jonah had to mull the possibilities over in his mind a bit, but finally agreed. "OK. Turn it over."

Sure enough, there was the dent Frank had made big as day.

"A mountain bike? A red one?"

"Whatever you want. Come on, I'll take you home. I'll need to explain this to your Dad. And you're gonna have to show me *exactly* where you found it."

"I can *tell* you where. It was shoved under the dock and covered with brush like I said."

"You mean the dock at the boat ramp?"

"No! The old boat landing that's falling in the lake. That's how I knew it was ditched. Nobody would stash a bike that nice under that rotten old landing if they wanted to use it again. It took me twenty minutes to dig it out."

"Was there a lock or a chain?"

"No! Just a lot of mud. I thought I'd never get it cleaned up."

"Tell me again, what landing?"

"The one in front of that rotten old building on Shoreline Drive."

Chapter 25

As he drove back to the lake, Lester realized that the new bike he had just promised Jonah would likely set him back a couple of hundred bucks. But it would be worth it to turn Brock's bike over to the sheriff, along with Jonah's explanation of where he had found it hidden. Although this evidence fell far short of proving Wickham's connection to Brock's appearance, Lester had a plan for closing that gap.

"Frank? It's Les. I need your help! Get your metal detector and meet me out front of your place in ten minutes." Lester ended the call and popped his cell phone in his shirt pocket without waiting for a response from Frank. When he arrived at Frank's place, the garage door was up revealing both cars, but Frank was nowhere to be seen. He pounded on the door until Gloria opened it. "Is Frank here?"

"Good afternoon to you too, Lester. Yes, he's out in the shed looking for something? What are you two up to now?"

"Uh, nothing much. I just called him and asked his help with the metal detector."

"Lose your wedding ring, did ya?"

"If you must know, yes. Yes I did." Lester lied as he buried his left hand suddenly in his pants pocket.

"I can see that," replied Gloria, looking him in the eye. "Lester Pierce, I've known you for more than 30 years. You're a lot of things, but a good liar isn't one of them. This has something to do with your obsession with Wickham and Brock's death doesn't it?"

Lester just looked past her and yelled, "Frank, are you coming or not?"

Gloria shrugged and warned, "You'd better not be getting him into anything dangerous or so help me..." Realizing her warning was of no use, she added, "Take your hand out of your pocket. You look silly and besides, if you fall over you'll break your wrist!"

Frank entered the patio door from the yard, metal detector in hand. "Found it. Just let me put in some fresh batteries and I'll be ready to go."

"You two be careful! And remember what I said, Lester!"

"Yes, mother!" Lester smiled as he held the door open for Frank.

As they reached Lester's truck, Frank asked, "Isn't that Brock's bike?"

"I'm certain it is. But I will still need to get the papers from Ashley to prove it." He proceeded to bring Frank up to speed on the whole bike recovery adventure, but when Lester explained where Jonah said he found the bike, Frank interrupted.

"You're going the wrong way! The dance hall is back there!"

"We're not going to the dance hall. We need to find where Brock left his bike before he disappeared. If my hunch is right, we'll need to look over on the other side of the lake."

Frank sat silently for a few moments as Lester's truck passed under the shade of several enormous cottonwood trees. "You're headed for Wickham's place, aren't you? You gotta let up on that and let the sheriff do his job."

"I know, but look at what he's accomplished so far. *I* found the bike, with your help of course. The sheriff didn't. *I* connected the dots about the CAFO and the dance hall, not the sheriff. I tell ya, he needs our help. I'll give him the bike and tell him everything I know, I just want to establish where the bike was when Brock last secured it, and I think I can with the help of your metal detector."

As Lester reached the stretch of road that passed in front of Wickham's stately acreage, he slowed to a crawl and scanned both sides of the road for a likely structure for securing a $1,500 bike. On the lakeside of the road for as far as he could see the only permanent structures were huge cottonwood trees with trunks far too large for Brock's bike cable. And Wickham's boat trailer was the only thing on the other side sturdy enough to attach a bike lock to. Lester parked the truck. "Are you gonna show me how this thing works?"

"It's real simple. Just turn it on like this, put on the head phones and wave it just above the ground. Where the tone gets the strongest, that's where you want to start digging."

Lester took the detector and stepped out of the truck. "OK, I know what I'm looking for. I'll take this side. You take the shore side and keep your eyes peeled for anything he could have fastened the cable to."

"I'll go as far as I can, but you know I don't have much wind power anymore. I may have to rest." Lester nodded his understanding and slipped the headset over his ears. For the next ten minutes, Lester trudged up and down the patch of tall, weedy grass on the road right-of-way on Wickham's side. Listening to the Theremin-like tones interspersed with clicks, he found nothing more than a few pop-top rings and a Roosevelt dime. He might have invested several more hours had it not been for the sudden appearance of one Lee Wickham, who wasted no time in expressing his displeasure.

"What the hell do you think you're doing?"

Lester, who had not actually heard Wickham's question due to the headphones, took them off and smiling his best fake smile greeted Wickham. "Oh hi Lee. Frank and I are just passing time looking for coins like the old retired farts we are."

Pointing toward Frank who had long ago taken up residence on a tree stump, Wickham observed, "Frank must be using a witching rod; I don't see a detector in his hands."

"Uh, we only have the one. We have to take turns."

"Well, you'll have to kill time somewhere else. You're on my property."

Lester could feel his dander rising. "Actually, I'm well within the *public* right of way, not your property, so...I don't need your permission."

"Well, I guess you've got me there. Technically the first 33 feet from the center of the road is public property. I don't own it. I don't pay taxes on it. I do have to maintain it however and I have the legal right to control access to it and I'm telling you again you need to get off of it. Now!"

Lester was never one to back down from a fight but he noticed a large bulge under Wickham's coat. Remembering Iowa's recently passed "stand your ground" law, he decided to back off before he got shot. He made no apology. "I see," was all he offered. "I guess Frank and I will have to confine our treasure hunt to the shoreline. Or are you claiming to own the whole damned lake, too?"

Wickham stared at Lester briefly before replying, "No. As long as you stay on that side of the road, there's nothing I can do about it. But if I see you over here again, I'll file trespassing charges. You two have a nice day."

"We'd better go, Lester. He's pretty pissed," Frank warned.

Lester did a double take as Frank rose from the stump and then redirected Frank pointing at the water's edge. "Don't look back. You hold the detector and I'll dig in the mud."

"What are you talking about Lester?"

"I'm sure he's watching us. Let's just poke around down here by the shore for a while to make it look good, and then we'll go." So the two old geezers trudged back and forth on the shoreline for the next half hour; Frank cluelessly carrying the detector and Lester occasionally digging in the mud for no particular purpose as far as Frank could see. Finally, Lester stretched his shoulders, arched his back and declared that they had had enough fun for one day. As they entered the truck, Frank demanded, "Les, what the hell was that all about?"

"Frank, my friend, we were looking for a place where Brock might have secured his bike."

"And we didn't find it."

"You're absolutely right. *We* didn't find it, but I'm pretty sure you *did*! The sap on the seat of your pants tells me that stump you were sitting on was freshly cut no more than a month ago. It was the only structure anywhere around small enough for the bike cable to fit around and still leave room for the bike."

"But we didn't find the cable."

"No, but we found something better. Unless Wickham is worried we'll find buried pirate treasure on his side of the road, I think we found more proof that he's hiding something. I'd bet anything that Wickham cut off the tree to free Brock's bike.

"Maybe so, but why didn't we find the cable? Even if he cut the tree to free the bike, he'd still had to have cut off the cable before the kid found it."

Lester chewed on that a while before answering. "Well, sure. But he could have done that anywhere after the bike was free. If he cut it right there he probably threw it right straight out into the lake as far as he could throw it. Or if he removed it in his house or garage, there's no telling where it wound up. But there's no way he would hang onto it."

"So we might never find it?"

"I'm not sure we need to anymore. Sure as hell he's hiding something and he just told us where to look. But right now I want to go look at some boats."

"Les, I think taking some time off from this would really do you some good, but before you go boat shopping, we need to see the sheriff and tell him what we know!"

"I'm not going to look at a boat to *buy*. I want to look at your wife's pictures to make sure I'm right about when that tree was cut down."

"And then you'll tell the sheriff?"

"First thing in the morning!"

Chapter 26

Lester knew that Ruthie closed the Coffee Spot every day as soon as the last customer left after the afternoon wave, so he wasted no time in dropping Frank off at his place. He then made a beeline for the Coffee Spot, pulling into the deserted parking area just as Ruthie exited the front door, keys in hand. He honked and made his way toward Ruthie as quickly as his 74-year-old legs would allow. "Ruthie, I need you to open up again."

"Coffee's all gone, and I'm all out of bait until the truck comes tomorrow afternoon," she explained as she moved away from the building.

"Doesn't matter, I just need to see Gloria's pictures."

"Lester Pierce, I know for a fact that you're not an art collector or a sailboat enthusiast. I don't know what else you're up to but surely it can wait until I open in the morning. My dogs are barking something fierce."

"If there's one thing I can't stand it's the sound of barking dogs. Let me in, and I'll give you a ride home. I wouldn't ask if it wasn't extremely important, Ruthie. I'll only be minute"

"OK, you had me at 'ride home', but make it quick. I appreciate the ride but what I really need is to soak my feet while I watch my soaps on the DVR."

As soon as the door was unlocked, Lester found the light switch and began examining each photo one at a time. "Well, I'll be a son of a bitch! Ruthie, you got a magnifying glass in here?"

"Lester Pierce, I'm warning you. NO! I don't have a magnifying glass or a microscope for that matter. What I do have is the Louisville Slugger I keep behind the counter for dealing with unruly fishermen. Now either whack yourself with it save me from having to get up or get your butt out that door and take me home! You can come back when I open at 5:30 tomorrow morning and spend all day staring at those pictures."

"Sorry, Ruthie. Thanks for your trouble."

He walked her to the truck and even opened the door for her. By the time they reached her home, she had mellowed somewhat. "What's so important about Gloria's pictures? You wanting to buy one to make up to Shirley for something?"

"No, I can't go into it, but I really needed to see something in one of them. Thanks again for letting me in. Maybe I'll go over to their house and get copies from Gloria."

"*There's* an idea! You have a nice evening and thanks for the lift home."

As he pulled into their driveway, Lester was as frustrated by what he knew as he was by the missing pieces. Gloria's photos had not only *not* cleared anything up, but had actually made things murkier. Although he couldn't be sure, in the dim light of the Coffee Spot it had appeared as though the small tree was present in a photo dated June 15th, but in the next photo dated June 19th it seemed to be gone. If Wickham had something to do with Brock's disappearance and death, why had he waited two weeks to cut down the tree? Maybe the others were right. Maybe he needed to turn the bike and everything else over to the sheriff and leave it to him. He plopped down in the most comfortable chair on the deck and threw his head back, rested his eyes and took a deep breath.

Before he had time to draw a second breath, Shirley slid open the patio door and demanded, "Lester Pierce have you two old farts been playing detective again?"

"No dear, why?"

"Don't lie to me. Gloria called right after you left with Frank."

"OK, I asked Frank to help me look into something, but it turned out to be a dead end. I'll take Brock's bike in to the sheriff in the morning and give him everything I have. I gave it my best shot, but I'm through."

Changing her tack slightly, Shirley asked, "How long has it been since you took me on a boat ride, just the two of us?"

"I don't know, last summer I suppose. Why?"

"Well, I think it's about time then. Take me out now."

"No, maybe tomorrow."

"Come on, it would help get your mind off all this stuff, help you relax. Help *us* relax."

He wasn't entirely sure what his wife meant by *relax*, but he couldn't think of any connotation that wouldn't be better than moping on the hot deck. "OK, we'll go. But I need to change and clean up first."

Noticing the mud on his shoes and knees for the first time, Shirley asked, "What in the world have you been...Never mind, I'd rather not know. Go get ready."

* * *

By the time they raised the Bimini top into position, killed all the spiders, swept the leaves and twigs from the deck and picked ants off of Shirley's life vest, Lester remembered why it had been so long since the pontoon had been used for anything other than tormenting fish. Shirley always enjoyed time on the boat. Eventually.

Once underway, Lester began to enjoy himself, as he always did on the boat. He had forgotten how relaxing it was to cruise slowly around the 450 acres of lake, just offshore. It provided a perfect vantage point from which to ogle the houses and cabins that surrounded Legion Lake. He was reminded how much he enjoyed the voyeuristic pastime of surveying his neighbors' maintenance responsibilities. Each time he saw a riding lawnmower traversing a neatly manicured lawn or some guy on his knees staining a deck, he took comfort in being a spectator and not a participant. Shirley, on the other hand, used the time to gather up new ideas for ways *they* could decorate, landscape or otherwise improve the aesthetic appeal of their own property. For her, the trek around the lake was sort of an old school Pinterest.

Eventually, their tour took them around to the far side of the lake. "Let's go out to the middle and open it up. The breeze will feel good," she suggested.

Lester knew she was trying to avoid Wickham's place and he knew why. She was trying to keep him from getting wound up again over Wickham – because she was worried about him and probably more than that, because she loved him. He knew all of that. And yet he steered the pontoon straight for Wickham's dock.

Shirley pleaded with him to veer the other direction. But, in a manner similar to a submarine captain on his way to torpedoing a German destroyer, he held true to the course and narrowly averted broadsiding Wickham's cabin cruiser. As they slid alongside the behemoth, he cut the motor and let their craft drift past Wickham's boat and the dock to which it was moored. As they passed the stern, they were so close they could have easily reached out and touched the hull. Shirley let out a shriek just in time to startle Wickham who had been enjoying a glass of wine on one of the benches of his enormous dock. He was so startled that he dropped the glass, shattering it on the carpeted boards beneath him.

"Oh, hi Lee. I hope we didn't scare you. Don't know what's got into this old tub. It just quit on me and left us adrift." Wickham, still too startled to form much of a response, only shook his head side to side and stared at the shards of glass surrounding his bare feet. "No, don't get up. I'm sure it will start again after awhile." And with that, Lester started the Evinrude with a single turn of the key. "See, we're good."

Lester revved the motor to full throttle and turned away from shore out toward the middle of the lake, waving goodbye over his shoulder to Wickham. Knowing he was likely in the deep stuff for what he had just done, Lester avoided eye contact with Shirley thinking it would be best to let her speak first. To his surprise, the only sound she made was a barely muffled sputter of derision. Realizing Shirley wasn't angered by his stunt but actually found some humor in it, Lester broke out into a big smile, followed by an actual laugh – the kind he hadn't had all summer. "You gotta admit, that was pretty funny!"

Shirley nodded in agreement, "Yes it was!" Suddenly sober however she added, "But it has to stop! Lester you have to leave the man alone and let the law deal with him." Although he wasn't ready to admit it, Lester knew she was right. In a rare move, he chose to exercise his right to remain silent. They continued on their tour of the lake, even cutting the motor again out in the center and drifting for a while. As he took a position on the bench behind the captain's controls, she quickly joined him. She took his weathered hand in hers and they sat silently listening to the geese and other water birds, watching the cloud formations. "I'm worried about you, mister. I know you want to help solve this, but I don't want you to get..." She couldn't bring herself to finish the thought, opting instead to squeeze his hand even more tightly.

"I know," he assured. Letting go of her hand, he put his arm around her and pulled her close to him. They enjoyed each other's presence for several more minutes in silence, each one thinking how long it had been since they had even held hands, let alone embraced.

Shirley finally broke the silence. "I know, let's go back to the cabin, and I'll make a romantic dinner. I still have time to run into town for a couple of sirloins and a bottle of wine."

Lester turned the key, revved the motor and headed straight for their dock. They held hands as he helped her up the stairs from the dock and all the way to the patio door of the cabin. Lester lifted the lid of the gas grill and cleaned the grate with a brush. "You sure you're OK going for stuff in town?"

"Oh, sure. You stay here and get the glasses and plates out and anything else we'll need. We can sit out on the deck until dark like we used to."

"Think we can stay awake that long?"

"So what if we can't? Last time I checked, the glider still held both of us and if we start to doze off, there's always the bed," she teased with a wink he hadn't seen in so long he almost missed it.

"OK, hurry back." He watched her car disappear down the road well out of eyesight before he pulled his phone out and dialed. "Hey Frank, it's Les. Are you still willing to help? I'll pick you up at nine in the morning. Bring all those flags you saved from the survey and make sure your phone's charged. And thanks, Frank. You won't regret this! Could you put Gloria on, I need to ask a favor." Lester looked out the window to make sure Shirley hadn't returned. "Say Gloria, do you two still have the Sunday paper? Good. Here's what I need you to do..."

Chapter 27

Perhaps it was the steak or maybe the wine. Or maybe, it was the sex. Whatever the reason, by the time the sports came on during the ten o'clock news Shirley was sawing logs. Lester on the other hand, was wide awake. And he didn't like it!

He couldn't decide. Either he was just keyed up about his plan for the next day, or he was feeling guilty about misleading Shirley about giving up on his search for the truth concerning Brock's death. Or maybe his encounters with Wickham were actually starting to spook him and he was getting cold feet. After staring at the moonlit ceiling of their bedroom for more than an hour, he decided he'd never been much good with multiple choice and did the only thing any red-blooded American man would do – he slipped out of bed, shut the bedroom door, opened a beer and turned on the TV. After twenty minutes of late night comedians, he was more than ready for sleep.

By the time the sun burst through the bedroom window and roused him from his dream, Shirley was already up. The smell of bacon and fresh coffee eventually won out over his desire for a few more minutes of pillow time. He pulled on some shorts and a t-shirt and emerged from the bedroom looking like a hungover college student who had already led a horribly hard life.

"You're up," he observed.

Shirley turned from the stove to look at him, smiled and said only, "Somebody had to make you your favorite breakfast." Extending her arms toward him for a hug, she kissed his cheek. "Did you have a good time last night?"

"Sure did!"

"I did too." She kissed him again, this time on the lips, before returning to the stove. "Thanks for the breakfast. I'm gonna grab a quick shower before I eat though. I'm supposed to have coffee with Frank at nine and then depending on how he feels, we might do something after lunch."

"Oh? When did you plan this?"

"Frank and I talked last night while you were in town. I thought as long as he was feeling good we should keep him active."

"Just you two? Not the wives?"

"No, I think Gloria has something this morning, but maybe this evening the four of us..."

"Not tonight! I plan to turn in early."

Thinking he should probably catch up on sleep himself he smiled and nodded his understanding. After a shower, he dressed for the day and rummaged through the computer desk until he located the flash drive and a magnifier, which he slipped into his pants pocket. Rejoining Shirley at the table, he expressed his appreciation for the breakfast and dove in. As he ate, Shirley reiterated her concerns about him continuing to provoke Wickham. As she pressed him for assurance that he would stay clear of the whole situation, Lester could feel his appetite slipping away. Finally he put down his fork and slid back from his half-eaten meal. Looking her in the eyes, he explained, "I want the same thing you do to come from this. I want to know what happened to Brock and who was responsible, whether that's Wickham or whoever. And I have no desire to wind up like Brock, so...just stop worrying, OK?"

Shirley appeared only slightly relieved by Lester's words, but she did give him a faint, "OK."

"I have to go pick up Frank. If he's up for it, we might have lunch as well so I don't know what time I'll be back. Go ahead and eat without me." He kissed her on the forehead and headed toward the door. Standing in the open door, he added, "I have no plans to be anywhere near Wickham today." He slid the patio door shut and climbed into his truck.

Shirley stood at the door and watched as he backed out of the driveway. *I hope for our sake that you know as much about Wickham as you think you do*, she thought.

Chapter 28

Frank was waiting in his driveway, clutching a handful of marker flags, when Lester pulled in. "Got your phone?"

"Yep."

"Is it charged?"

"Yep. And I brought the flags. What do we need them for?"

"I stopped at the Coffee Spot yesterday and looked at Gloria's photos. Even though they all have the shore on Wickham's side of the lake in the background, I couldn't make any sense out of when that tree was cut down. And the more I thought about the pictures, something bothered me. I want to go study them again and then you and I are going to use the flags to reconstruct a crime scene."

Frank's face lit up. "Just like on *CSI*?"

"Yep, just like on *CSI*. Except without the good-looking women."

"Or the handsome young men," Frank chuckled.

"Yeah, what is it they say? Old age and treachery will always trump youthful inexperience?"

"Huh?"

Retrieving the flash drive from his pocket and ignoring Frank's question, he asked, "You know how to use Gloria's camera, right?"

"Sure. I set it up for her right out of the box and helped her learn to run it."

"OK, I want you to take this drive and load all of her pictures that have anything to do with the lake area onto it and get it back to me. Will you do that?"

"Sure, if it's OK with her. They're her pictures."

"I know, but you can't ask her. Both of our wives are about to kill us over this. You are not taking the pictures, you are just copying them and I'm not going to do anything with the pictures except look at them. But, if I'm right, there's something on her camera that will crack this thing open." Frank, as usual, had to think awhile, but finally answered in the affirmative.

By the time they pulled into the parking lot of the Coffee Spot, over a dozen cars and pickups were already there. "I hope the cinnamon rolls aren't gone," Frank said with a worried look.

"When we get inside you go ahead and order what you want, on me. If the rolls are gone, get something else and I'll owe you double next time. And take a table in the back." Frank did he was as asked while Lester examined each photo carefully. Taking two off their hooks on the wall, he approached Ruthie. "So you decided to buy a couple after all. Gloria will be thrilled. That'll set ya back 40 bucks."

"Actually, I don't think she'd be all that thrilled if the only ones that sold were bought by a friend. I just need to borrow these for a few hours. I can have them back before closing."

"I don't think I can let you do that without Gloria's approval."

"Oh, she's already given permission. I thought Frank explained that."

Ruthie looked at Frank from across the room. Frank waved and nodded his approval of the cinnamon roll that filled his pie hole. "Well, OK. If Frank's alright with it I am too, but you have them back on the wall in the same shape they're in now by two o'clock or I'll come looking for you." She reached under the counter for the bat just to make her point.

"Got it. Will do!" He helped himself to a big cup of coffee and a roll and joined Frank at the table but ignored both as he poured over the photos with the magnifier.

"What are you looking for?"

"I'm still not sure, but I think we'll know by this afternoon. Finish your roll and then I'll run you over to Wickham's place," Lester directed.

"Me? Aren't you gonna be there with me, too? What if he raises hell again?"

"First of all, I need to be back here. And you can forget about Wickham for today, he's in Iowa City."

"How do you know that?"

"Because Gloria and I made sure he went over there to show a couple of houses."

Chapter 29

Before dropping Frank off, Lester made a couple of passes by Wickham's place, even pulling into the drive at one point. At no time was there any sign of life or any sign of either Wickham or his wife. Satisfied that it was safe, Lester handed Frank a marker pen and let him out by the boat trailer directly in front of the house. "When I get back over to the Beer Garden, I'll call your cell. I'm sure you won't be seeing anything of Wickham, but if anything happens that you don't want to handle just pretend to be out for a walk and call me. I'll come right over and get you."

Lester wasted no time in making his way back to the Beer Garden on the shore in front of the Coffee Spot. He took the binoculars from the door of his truck and walked up and down the shore looking first at one of the photos and then through the binoculars across the lake at Frank. Eventually he slid a picnic table from the Beer Garden to a position a few yards to the East and placed the photos on it. Sitting facing the lake, he looked at the first photo with the magnifier and then called Frank. "OK, you need to stand on Wickham's side of the road in line with the trailer, facing the lake, and listen carefully to my directions."

"Got it." Frank moved into position as directed.

Lester put his phone on speaker and observed Frank through the binoculars. "OK, move about five feet to the right." Lester checked the photo again. "One more foot to the right." Frank complied. "That's it. Mark that flag #1 and stick it in the ground right there." Again Frank did as requested. Lester examined the second photo and spotted Frank through the binoculars. "OK, now move about 25 feet to your left, about eight paces." He checked the photo again and again found Frank through the lens of the binoculars. "No, a couple feet more to the left. That's it! Mark a flag #2 and put it right there. Don't move either of them and I'll be right over.

It was all Lester could do to keep the truck under the speed limit of 25 mph as he drove back to join Frank. The excitement of knowing that he was surely onto something helpful suddenly gave way to stark fear as he spotted Wickham's huge Escalade parked by the old dance hall and two men – one of which looked a lot like Wickham – walking down the hill toward the lake. "What the hell is he doing at the lake?" Lester asked out loud. Slowing to a stop, he backed down the road until he was even with the Escalade and hidden from Wickham's view by the dance hall ruins. He looked both ways to make sure no one was watching and knelt on one knee next to the rear tire on the driver's side. He unscrewed the valve stem cap, put a tiny pebble inside it and replaced it turning it slowly until he heard a very satisfying his'. He re-entered his truck and continued on around the lake toward Frank. As he watched the Escalade disappear in his rearview mirror, he laughed out loud remembering when he had done the same thing to his high school principal's tire nearly 60 years earlier. "*And old man Riley said nothing good would ever come of doing that,*" he chuckled.

When he reached Frank, he was literally standing on one leg and then the other. "Thank God you're here. Are we done yet? I gotta piss."

Motioning toward the trees by the lake shore he explained, "You're gonna have to use one of nature's toilets, we're not done yet and we're running outta time." He didn't tell Frank about Wickham to save the time and the effort of more explanations. Standing across the road from the trailer, he studied the positions of the flags relative to the trailer. He cursed under his breath about not making any sense of information he had been so sure of 30 minutes earlier. Frank returned from his nature call, muttering something which Lester completely ignored.

He retrieved his tape measure from the toolbox in his truck and measured the overall length of the trailer. He had Frank hold the end of the tape as he measured from the tip of the tongue to the axels: 22 feet. They measured the overall length: 35 feet. He numbered two more flags and sent Frank with the end of the tape to the first flag. Lester stuck a flag in at the 35-foot mark. Then he moved to the 22-foot mark and attempted to insert a flag. But no matter where he tried, the ground beneath the tall grass was too hard. Perplexed again, he stood in his tracks and tried to make sense of what he knew. "Shh…listen. Do you hear that?"

"Sounds like water running."

"I know, but from where?" Lester kicked at the dirt and gravel beneath his feet, until he uncovered the edge of a large piece of metal. "Go get me the tire iron, Frank." When Frank returned, Lester had kicked off enough dirt and gravel to reveal a huge manhole cover.

"I think it's a storm sewer."

"That's probably what goes to the flap gate down by the shore," Frank observed, pointing.

"The *what*?"

"The metal cover that keeps animals out of the storm sewer. I saw it just now when I was down there."

Lester stood, hands on his hips, and stared at the manhole cover for several seconds before he spoke. "OK, so why did Wickham move his trailer just far enough to park the wheels on top of the manhole? And then move it back where it was a week later?"

"Maybe to mow?"

Turning to face him, Lester said, "Frank, this grass hasn't been mowed…" but he stopped short when he saw the Hank's Tire Service truck on the opposite shore headed toward the old dance hall. "Oh shit! I think it's time to call the sheriff."

Twelve minutes later, the county sheriff pulled onto the shoulder across from the trailer. Emerging from the car, his face was nearly as red as the flashing lights atop his cruiser.

"What in the name of hell have you done? If I find you've disturbed a crime scene…"

Frank turned and walked briskly away.

"Where you going?"

"I was just walking by."

"Frank, get back here!" barked Lester.

Chapter 30

And thus began Lester's long, convoluted justification about why he had been called the sheriff and how he came to be in possession of Brock's bike. The sheriff took particular interest in Lester's use of Gloria's pictures to document the position of the boat trailer and although he was nearly as puzzled about Wickham's reasons for moving it, he was not as suspicious as Lester. Whether Lester convinced the sheriff or maybe just wore him down, either way the sheriff eventually calmed down and agreed that Lester and Frank had moved the case forward somehow. He was about to call in his crime scene unit when an approaching car screeched to a stop a quarter of a mile away and turned around in the road.

"That's Wickham!" Lester shouted as the Escalade peeled out and sped away in the opposite direction.

"What the hell? Dispatch, issue a BOLO for a silver Escalade with a Linn county plate registered to a ..." looking to Lester.

"Lee Wickham. Or maybe Aspen Properties."

"Lee Wickham or Aspen Properties. It's headed east out of the Legion Lake area. Intercept and hold Mr. Lee Wickham for questioning." The sheriff removed his hat and wiped his brow. "Now show me where you think he parked the trailer." Lester directed the sheriff to the 22-foot flag and kicked at the gravel to reveal even more of the manhole cover. "And you think this proves *what*?"

"I think it's suspicious that Brock's bike turned up buried under property tied to Wickham and I think he moved the trailer to hide something. He sure didn't move it to mow."

"Well, that all seems pretty circumstantial, but let's just open this baby up and see what's down there."

The sheriff wedged the tire iron under one edge and pried it loose from the collar. They slid it clear of the opening far enough to peer into the dark cavity below. Lester turned on the flashlight app on his cell phone. As he shone the light down the ladder, it quickly illuminated a form that even Lester had not expected. As the hair on the back of his neck stood up, Lester nearly dropped his phone down the hole. "Oh my God!" was all he could say.

"What is it?" demanded the sheriff.

"It looks like a backpack to me; an *orange* backpack... Just like the one Brock was wearing the last time I saw him!"

"How can you be so sure that it's his?"

"You're right. It's probably one of the hundreds of orange backpacks that have gone missing around here this summer!" Lester rose to his feet. "Don't you see? That's why Wickham parked the trailer on top of the manhole – to hide evidence!"

Frowning at Lester, the sheriff made a second call on his radio. "Dispatch, hold the driver of the silver Escalade for questioning and send the evidence team to...1021 Lakeview Road at Legion Lake." Turning back to Lester he asked, "OK, we'll check this out, but I think it's mighty interesting that you looked at a couple of pictures hanging on the wall and immediately conclude that this Wickham fella killed Brock Sanford."

"I never said that! But I have always thought he was involved somehow."

"And why was that?"

"From the very beginning, Brock was helping to lead the fight against Wickham's CAFO plans. He stood up to him at the public meeting, and got people out here riled up about the CAFO plans. That had to have pissed Wickham off."

"Don't stop now, Columbo. I wanna hear the part of this fairytale where you tell me about the evidence you have that Wickham did something worse than move his own boat trailer for Christ's sake!"

"What about the bike? Brock never would have left his bike unattended – it's worth a fortune. He always locked it up with a cable lock. The only thing around here small enough to get that cable around would have been that little tree down by the shore and it got cut down after Brock went missing. That's why I started looking at the pictures in the first place; I was trying to confirm exactly when the little tree was cut down."

"And did you?"

"No. There weren't enough pictures. I only narrowed it down to about two weeks."

"You know as well as I do that he could have parked that bike anywhere around the lake or even in town. We have no idea where he rode off to."

"What about his backpack? If someone stole his bike from somewhere in town, what would the likelihood be they would come all the way out here to dispose of the backpack and then crawl down a manhole and hang it on the ladder?"

Seeing that Lester was right, the sheriff scowled and snapped back, "Well if you're right, you'd better pray that you haven't compromised any evidence while you've been playing Dick Tracy!"

"I thought he was Columbo?" Frank said, looking innocent.

"Look, the last time I spoke to Brock, on the morning of the day he disappeared, he told me he was heading out to collect more lake water samples. He was trying to find the source of some kind of contaminant…e-something or other. He said he was focusing on this side of the lake."

"E. coli?"

"Yeah, that. He said he'd narrowed it down to this side and needed to collect several more samples to pinpoint the source. I have all his data in my truck."

"What are *you* doing with it?"

"Brock was working up information about the lake and the environmental impact the CAFO would have on it. He was supposed to meet with the guy from ICEP and give it to him. But, when he didn't show, Ashley searched their cabin for me and couldn't find any sign of it. All she found was his E. coli data."

"Whoa, you searched his cabin?"

"No, I asked Ashley to find his CAFO presentation. If that's his backpack, I'd bet my next Social Security check that it has sample bottles and the CAFO presentation in it."

The sheriff paced alongside the trailer and then turned to look across the lake. "Those pictures were taken from that little bait shop over there?"

"Yep."

"And you figured out the location of the trailer from those pictures?"

"Yep."

He removed his hat again, ran his hand over the top of his head, down the side of his face stopping finally at his chin. Making eye contact with Lester, he asked, "I have to say, you've drawn some interesting conclusions. What's your background?"

"We watch a *lot* of *CSI!*" Frank answered proudly. "*You* should check it out."

Chapter 31

"Look, how many times do I have to tell you? I had nothing to do with it!" Wickham shouted.

"As many times as it takes until my questions have all been answered," replied the deputy.

"What questions? What else can I possibly tell you?"

"Well, for example, I'd like to understand why you moved your boat trailer in the middle of the season."

"My boat trailer? What does that have to do with anything?"

"It just seems odd that you chose to back it up in the middle of the season and then pull it back where it was a week later."

Wickham's face showed the first signs of relief as he answered, "I needed the room for a delivery truck that was coming."

"To deliver what?"

"Furniture. From Amana."

"You made them park down *there* and carry furniture up the hill?"

"It was just a grandfather clock! One trip, two men, it was done."

"Why not just let them back up your driveway?"

"I didn't want that huge truck cracking the new concrete we'd just poured this spring."

The deputy looked at the sheriff who frowned and shook his head slightly. Sliding a pad of paper and a pen across the table to Wickham, the deputy informed Wickham, "I'm gonna need the name of the shop that delivered the clock and the date."

"I don't remember the exact date."

"Make your best guess. Don't worry, we'll check it out with the Amana shop."

Wickham scrawled the information on the pad and slid it back. "Can I go now?"

"We still..." started the deputy.

Touching the deputy's arm, the sheriff interrupted, "I think that's all we need for now, Mr. Wickham." Rising to his feet, he added, "You're free to go." Scowling, Wickham pushed back from the table and headed toward the door. "Oh, just one more thing, Mr. Wickham. I know you travel a fair amount in your profession. Just make sure you don't take any *long* trips, you know, like outside the state of Iowa, until we resolve this matter."

His face contorting into a sneer, Wickham quickly exited the room and slammed the door. "Is that it? You just turned him loose? I have a lot more questions for him!" the deputy complained.

"So do I, but let's see what he does next, after he's had a chance to sweat about this. Meanwhile, why don't you take a quick trip over to the Amana colonies and find out everything you can about that delivery? I'll call the State DCI again and see if I can speed up the coroner's report. Once I have that, I think this whole thing will make a lot more sense."

Once back in his vehicle, Wickham pulled out of the parking lot onto the street and headed off into the setting sun. He slowed at the first cross street and turned right. Checking the rear view mirror, he came to a full stop in the middle of the block. He pounded his fist on the steering wheel and cursed at the top of his lungs, "Goddamn it! That stupid little son of a bitch!" Putting his hand to his face, he felt the stubble of his five o'clock shadow and considered the hot mess he was in. His funk was briefly interrupted when the driver behind him honked impatiently. As the light at the approaching intersection turned yellow, he pulled over to the curb and made a call. When the receptionist answered, he demanded, "I need to see Paul ASAP. It's very important!"

"Mr. Welch has a two o'clock opening tomorrow."

"I need to see him today!"

"I'm sorry, but he's in court the rest of the day, and again tomorrow morning."

"Well, get a message to him that I need to meet with him as soon as he's out of court today! It's urgent!"

"What shall I say this is regarding?"

Wickham's next words reflected a level of honesty he was unaccustomed to and the tears that accompanied them revealed that he was beginning to understand just how badly screwed he was. "Tell him it's a...criminal matter. I think...I... Just tell him!" Hanging up he completed his thought silently. *I think I killed someone!* Then, in the middle of a hot Iowa summer day, the real estate mogul of Legion Lake sat silently in his Escalade and wept.

Chapter 32

"Don't forget the coffee this time!" Lester yelled to Frank trudging away from the pontoon toward the red Chevy.

Frank swatted the air with his left hand and reached for the truck door with the other. He zipped his jacket and turned the collar up to ward off the chilly autumn air.

Lester transferred the gas from the can into the tank and untied the ropes that tethered the beaten, old pontoon to the dock getting ready for the last fishing run of the season. As he turned the motor over, he shaded the rising sun from his eyes with his hand and yelled to Frank, "Come on, they're not gonna wait all day!"

Grabbing the railing just in time, Frank shoved off and grumbled, "It's the last week of October, for Christ's sake. They're done waiting. The smart ones have already found a nice warm place to hole up for the winter." The pontoon slid away from the dock as the old Evinrude wound up to full speed. "That's what *we* should be doing!"

"Would you stop your bitchin'? I just thought we should have one last run at it. You know, for the season."

"I shouldn't even be out here, a man in my condition."

"Your *condition*? Listen to you. You'd think you were..." Lester looked at his friend of more than 30 years and then shifted his gaze to the opposite side of the boat. "Ah hell, what do they know anyway?"

"They know enough, I reckon."

Giving his captain's duties his full attention, Lester turned a wide arc and slowed to trolling speed. Baiting a jig, he cast over the stern and watched the drops of water glistening in the morning sun on the monofilament line. Setting the pole down, he gave the wheel a slight correction and reached for a second pole. After casting it over the stern he handed it to Frank.

"So how you been feeling? Sleeping OK?"

"Good as I can, I expect. Coughing a lot at night. Gloria moved to the other bedroom so at least she gets some sleep."

"You two ought to go south, maybe to Florida...or Phoenix."

Frank turned to look at Lester, rolling his eyes. "Ain't it bad enough I'm dying? You want me to do it among those idiots?"

"Stop saying that! You're gonna be fine."

"Les, I think this thing's bothering you more than it is me! I can't live forever, gotta go sometime."

Lester drew a long breath and bit his lower lip, but his pensive look turned to a smile. "Speaking of 'gotta go,' remember that time you had to piss so bad you hung it over the rail and you didn't see that gal in the wood strip canoe until she was right on us?"

Frank's face broke into a smile, his first all morning. "Yeah, she got a good eyeful. I sort of spoiled her for any other guy, I reckon," he remembered proudly.

"Or that time I was hauling them in two at a time and you weren't even getting a bite. You got so mad you threw your tackle box in the lake and forgot your cell phone was in it?"

"Well, at least I know enough to bring in a stringer before I put the boat on the trailer and drag it all the way back home. People in town are still talking about how big those fish heads were that you caught," Frank reminded.

Lester thought of a juicy reply, but kept it to himself as Frank's laughter turned to hacking and coughing.

"You gonna be OK? You want me to pound on your back or anything?"

Frank held up a cautionary hand and shook his head. When he could speak again he said, "Just don't make me laugh anymore."

"You want a beer?"

"Can't, remember? Meds." Frank explained.

Lester reached for the thermos and poured a cup of coffee. He passed it to Frank who poured himself a cup. They sat silently and nursed the coffee, each man sure he knew what the other was thinking. Frank finally broke the silence. "It won't be long now."

"Frank! Come on, man. Think positive!" More deafening silence as each man choked down his own thoughts by inspecting his reel and gazing over the stern at the line as it disappeared under the water. Just then the drag on Frank's pole began to sing as he first tugged on it and then released it. Cutting the motor, Lester rose to a crouch and then stood up straight. "What is it? Have you hooked old Wally?"

"I think so! Give me a hand, will ya? Where's the net?"

Lester scanned the floor in vain looking for the landing net. "I think I left it in the truck. Didn't think we'd need it," he explained sheepishly.

Frank frowned at him. "Yep...Mr. Positive!" he said shaking his head.

As Frank cranked the reel to narrow the gap between the fish and the boat, Lester pulled on the line allowing no slack. Slowly, the business end of the line emerged from the green, brackish water. "It's him! You hooked old Wally! I think he's grown even bigger!"

Frank peered over the rail and beamed with pride. "Well, I'll be...I never thought I'd see *him* again. What're we gonna do?"

"Well you gotta release him. I mean it's old Wally! You gotta leave him here so you can catch him again next year."

"You take the bucket out front and when I get him around to you, scoop him up."

"You aren't gonna keep him are you?" Lester demanded.

"Go on, get out front with the bucket."

Taking the bucket, Lester knelt on the front platform and watched as Frank towed Old Wally up to the front of the boat. Frank pulled Wally's head up out of the water and ordered, "Get the bucket in the water behind him and when I yell, scoop him up."

Positioning himself, Lester crouched like a sprinter waiting for the gun. "Now!" Frank shouted. In one smooth motion, Lester scooped Wally from the water and set him onto the deck of the pontoon. The monster fish thrashed in the bucket, sloshed most of the water out onto Lester, and made him look as though he had just wet himself. In an exercise in futility, he brushed himself off then scowled at Frank and asked, "Got any more bright ideas?" Frank could only point at Lester's crotch and cough.

Lester made his way back to the controls, cussing Frank as he went. Frank stood over the bucket, admiring Wally, and ignoring Lester's review of his pedigree. "I say we call it a day," Lester said as he turned the key and waited for the familiar sputter of the Evinrude. All he heard was the whine of the starter. "Choke it," Frank offered, as he worked to remove the hook from Wally's mouth.

"I did."

"Squeeze the bulb then."

"I know how to start my own motor!"

More whining from the starter. "Apparently not," Frank observed. "We better call Ed for a tow. Give me your phone."

"Use your own damn phone!" Lester snapped.

"Can't. Left it in the truck. Thought it'd be safer there. Come on, give me yours and I'll call Ed."

Lester continued cranking for a few more seconds and then explained, "It's on the charger…in the truck."

Frank turned and looked straight at Lester, "Well, that's just great! What am I supposed to do now?"

"You? I'm the one freezing my family jewels off."

"Well, I want to go in. Now!"

"Then you'd better shoot off a flare or start waving, cause this beast ain't gonna start."

"OK, give me your jacket so I got something to wave."

Lester ignored him and used the horn to issue three short toots, three long ones and three more short ones.

"What's that?"

"It's S.O.S. You know, Morse code."

"So we're gonna be rescued by a telegrapher or maybe a passing boy scout?"

"Every boater knows it…it's right in the damn boating manual. Just shut up and keep waving!"

Frank held his hand over his brow and squinted as he surveyed the panorama of the lake. "I think we're the only ones out here, Les. Might as well save the battery until we see someone."

Lester stopped honking and scanned the lake for other boats.

"Son of a bitch!"

"I think we're drifting toward the north shore. We'll probably be within earshot of those docks in an hour or so," Frank observed.

Lester wet his index finger in his mouth and held it up. "We're definitely heading that way, but who knows how long it will take."

After several minutes silently watching for boats, Frank cautiously offered, "We're quite a team, huh, Les?"

"What do ya mean?"

"Well, I was just thinking. We've been fishing together for what...30 years?

"I think we started in '87 when you and Gloria first bought out here. We've had some great times all right."

More silence. Frank cleared his throat and finally said, "I never told you thanks."

"For what? I've got a boat and you don't. You buy your share of gas and beer and bait. No thanks necessary."

"I don't mean for *that*." Frank paused as he looked down at the frayed carpet beneath his feet. "I mean for being my friend. Thirty years is a long time to stick with a person, especially me. You and Shirley have been great to Gloria and me. That's all. I mean you've stuck with us through this whole cancer thing."

"Well, what the hell did you expect us to do? That's what friends do, Frank."

"I know, and you've done it. You've been great! That's all I'm saying."

"OK. I get it. Thanks back at you."

Frank nodded as he cleared his throat and then began another round of hacking. As the coughing subsided, he pulled a crumpled red hankie out of his pocket and wiped his eyes. Lester did the same using the sleeve of his jacket.

"One more thing," Frank added. "We are gonna go on a trip...south. Gloria booked us a condo for the winter on South Padre Island. She insisted we take one last trip. We're leaving Wednesday."

Lester sat frozen as he took the bulletin in and ran the numbers in his head. "Well, that's great! It should be great for you. Get out of the Iowa cold and relax in the sun." Lester forced a smile. "So when will you guys return?"

"Steve and Sharon and the kids are gonna join us for Thanksgiving and again for Christmas."

"Oh, that's really gonna be nice. So, you'll be back up here for Easter?"

"Gloria booked the condo right through the end of April."

"Well, that way you can get out here just in time for the start of the crappie run. Perfect!"

"And I went to the doctor on Thursday. He found some more spots." Frank's voice trailed off as tears began to flow. "He says three, maybe six months...tops."

Lester stood and reached for his old friend's shoulder. Helping him to his feet, he wrapped his arms around him and hugged him tightly. When Frank could speak again, he explained, "I want to be near the kids until the end. They can't come up here, cause you know, work and stuff."

"Oh...sure...that's what you *need* to do. I understand," Lester said ignoring the sound of a boat motor in the distance.

"I wanted to tell you sooner, but...well...I didn't know..."

"Oh, no...I understand," Lester assured him again, wiping his eyes on his sleeve.

Frank rose to his feet and looked at Wally once again. "Look at him, if he's lucky, someday somebody will keep him, mount him and hang him up on a wall, maybe at Ruthie's place. Then people will know of him forever." Old Wally thrashed around in the bucket, nearly escaping. "It's different for people. We start out young, just like the fish, and as kids we can't wait to get older so we can work, or drive or you know...have sex. We have things we're curious about. But we just get older and older 'til finally we're *too* old; too old to work, too old to drive, even too old to screw. Eventually there's nothing to look forward to any more, except..."

"There's always Viagra."

"Well sure, that stuff puts the lead in your pencil, but what good is that if she's stopped wanting to read what you can write?"

This gave Lester a brief chuckle until he considered how accurate Frank's observation was.

"So you want to keep him and have him mounted?"

"No! He's still got things to look forward to."

"So what *are* you saying? You thinking of having yourself stuffed when the time comes?"

"No, I'm just saying that eventually we don't have anything to look forward to except the end and whatever comes after that, that's all. And now that the end's in sight...I'm getting...curious...again."

Lester paused to consider what his old friend had just laid on him; Frank realizing he had just touched on the profound, quickly changed the subject back to the trophy fish at hand. Picking the bucket up by the bail he headed out onto the front platform. "Help me turn him loose. I don't wanna hurt him. Maybe you'll think of me whenever you hook him."

Lester jumped up and steadied Frank as he dropped to one knee. Frank lowered the bucket into the water and turned it on its side allowing Wally to swim away.

"I'll miss you old fella," Frank uttered solemnly.

"Me too," Lester whispered, looking at Frank through tear-filled eyes.

"Hey, look! A boat!" Frank shouted. With that, Lester returned to the horn as Frank waved his arms. The boat appeared to be headed straight for them. "Looks like we're gonna get a tow."

They strained to make out the driver, but neither of them recognized her or the boat. As the boat turned to come alongside, the woman yelled, "I've been watching you through my binoculars ever since the first S.O.S. You two twinks need a tow?"

Bristling at her insinuation, Lester blurted, "I'll have you know this guy's hung like a horse!"

Frank swatted him away with his hand.

"I know!" replied the woman with a smile. "I'm usually out here in a wood strip canoe."

Chapter 33

Winter always took its toll on Lester and Shirley's little piece of heaven. As the sun illuminated the yard surrounding the cabin Lester could see the past winter had left its marks. Dead leaves matted the grass, dead limbs littered the lawn and the TV antenna was missing most of its crossbars, a sure sign that Shirley would finally get the dish service she had been insisting on for the past two years. So it was that on the last week of April, Lester looked over his domain and across the lake to the far shore. The For Sale sign in front of Wickham's place brought him no pleasure, only relief as he recounted the ways Wickham's plans had crumbled. He almost felt sorry for the jerk...almost.

He took another sip from his coffee and reviewed the list of jobs that surely awaited him before dark. Always a big believer in the power of skillful neglect, he decided to tackle the easiest first and stepped off the deck in the direction of the mailbox. Cleaning out a winter's worth of junk mail was certainly one of the least objectionable tasks on the list. The mailman seemed to take pleasure in stuffing the box with all manner of flyers, ads, shoppers and such every winter and, opening the mailbox door, Lester could see he had outdone himself this winter. The only part of the task that took any skill whatsoever was carefully going through the pieces just to make sure nothing of actual importance was hidden between the layers. Lester clutched the bundle under his left arm, zipped his coat all the way up with his right and hunkered into the wind on his way to the fire pit. He intended to set fire to the entire lot, but realized he had no matches and changed course toward the deck. He slid the patio door shut and plopped the bundle of mail on the table. As his eyes adjusted to the bright light, he made out the steam from two mugs of coffee waiting on the table – Shirley's favorite mug and the one Frank had given him after winning it in the fishing derby.

Then he realized that Shirley was standing in the kitchen doorway clutching her cell phone to her chest. Seeing the tears on her cheeks, he asked the question, even though he knew the answer, "Bad news?"

"It was Gloria...Frank's gone! She said he passed away in his sleep last night!"

"No! I thought the cancer center told them..." Lester swallowed hard and reached out to Shirley guiding her into a chair at the table. "How's Gloria?"

"Steve and Sharon and the kids are with her. She seemed good, considering."

Lester reached for the handle of his coffee mug, but held on without lifting it from the table. "Anything about services?"

"That's up in the air. They're all still in Texas."

He released the mug handle and reached across for Shirley's hand as he joined her at the table. The two sat silently for a few moments, each trying to take in the news.

"Of course, we need to be there," Shirley reminded Lester. "You'll probably be a pall bearer."

"Sure, if they need me. They have lots of friends back there. And a big family."

Shirley studied the coffee in her half-filled cup as Lester opened the bundle of mail and flipped through it. He thumbed its leaflets and flyers without actually processing the pages; his thoughts were on his friend of more than 30 years and the fact that he had seen him for the last time. They had shared their last beer. They would never go fishing for Old Wally again.

"You know, I've had a lot of friends over the years come and go, but, right now, I feel like Frank was my only one."

"Les, you know that's not true, you have lots..."

The frown on Lester's face as he cleared his throat and began to speak again stifled Shirley mid-sentence. "It's not only true, it's my fault. Over the years I've pushed them away as they did something to piss me off. One by one, I cut them off like you prune your roses."

As much as Shirley wanted to disprove Lester's point, her silence only helped to make it for him. Taking scant notice, Lester continued,

"It's been different with Frank. He's ticked me off plenty of times, but I always forgave him. We were still...we still ARE friends!"

As his eyes filled with tears, he could no longer tell one piece of mail from the next. He rose from the table and quickly exited the cabin. Barely able to see, he trudged the familiar path to the dock as Shirley watched him, uncertain what he would do next. By the time he reached the shore and the mooring for the docks, he had all but run out of steam. He stood on the edge of the dock motionless except for the heaving of his shoulders and chest as he sobbed. Only then did he realize he still clutched his empty coffee mug. He looked at its murky outline briefly and then winding up, threw it far out into the waters of Legion Lake. Instantly, he regretted his actions. But, as he stood there, he reconsidered and a slight smile came to his lips as he realized that was probably what Frank had done...with his tackle box...with his phone inside.

"Lester, come here." Shirley called to him from the cabin doorway. Wiping his eyes with his sleeve, he turned and saw Shirley waving an envelope in the air. "You have a letter...from Frank!"

As he made his way back up the bank to the cabin, Lester stopped midway to catch his breath and ponder the events of the past few minutes. Even before he was back in the cabin he asked, "Well, what did he say?"

"I haven't opened it. It's addressed to you, marked 'PERSONAL.' "

Lester's brow furrowed briefly, as he took the envelope from Shirley. It was postmarked "South Padre Island, TX 78597." He held it up to the light and could tell it contained a photo in addition to a letter.

"I found it buried in the bundle of junk mail. I think it came two weeks ago."

Still puzzled, Lester cautiously tore the end off of the envelope and blew gently into the opening. As he shook the envelope open, he freed the hand-written letter and a snapshot from inside. The photo was a group shot of Steve, Sharon and their three kids gathered around Frank. He looked pale and thin, but happy. He sported a big grin and a yarmulke, and an Easter basket was on his lap, courtesy of the grandkids, probably. An oxygen tank sat at his feet, the hose barely visible on his cheeks and under his nose. Lester laid the photo on the table and silently read Frank's letter.

Dear Lester:

As you can see from our Easter Sunday picture, I'm still alive although not well. We have had a very good winter here in the warmth of Texas. It has been great to spend this time with Steve and his family. I wish we could see you and Shirley again, but I suppose we won't, or at least I won't.

Lester, you have been a great friend! We both really appreciate everything you've done for us over the years, especially this last one. When Gloria comes out to the lake this spring, she'll probably need some help with the place and I know she can count on you two if she needs anything. Because of you and Shirley, all those years at the lake were really fun! If it hadn't been for the Pierces, we'd probably have been bored out of our minds years ago. Thank you again for being such wonderful friends.

Yours,

Frank Mariboe

P.S.: I also need to thank you for everything you did with that Wickham thing. From the beginning, you knew what to do about that bastard. I tried to help out as much as I could. I hope I did right. There's no such thing as a free lunch, right?"

Lester sighed heavily and looked at the picture again and then held it up for Shirley to see.

"Nice photo of the family, except Gloria's not in it. She must have taken it," Shirley observed.

"Yeah, I guess somebody had to take it. Probably Gloria; it's got that little date thing in the corner like her..." Lester stopped mid-sentence and thought for several seconds, looking first at the picture and then at the letter in his hand and then the picture again. Suddenly he asked, "When was that envelope postmarked?"

"April 15th, two weeks ago like I said. Why?"

Taking the phone from his pocket, he checked for the date and found it to be April 28th. Checking the picture again, he couldn't believe his eyes. The date time stamped in the lower right hand corner was clearly April 30.

"What is it, Les?"

"Oh, nothing. I...just misread this I guess." Lester quickly scooped up the picture and letter and put both back into the envelope, which he tucked safely in his shirt pocket.

He sat staring into space for a few minutes until Shirley interrupted his thoughts to ask, "More coffee?" He gave no answer. "Les, do you want more coffee? Or some breakfast?"

"Huh? Oh, no thanks. I'd better get back to work so we can pick up and go when we find out about Frank's services." Gathering the pile of junk mail, he took the box of safety matches from the mantle and headed out the patio door, pausing in the opening. "This has been such a hard year for Gloria, hasn't it?"

"It was hard on all of us, first Brock then Frank's cancer and now this. Things have got to get better this summer, don't they?"

"You're right...I sure intend to try to make them better." Shutting the door behind him, he headed to the fire pit and placed the bundle of junk mail in the center. He gathered the fallen branches from throughout the yard and placed them on top of the pile. He struck a match on the side of the box and touched it to the edges of some of the newsprint. The flames quickly spread to the remainder of the pile. Retrieving the envelope from his shirt again, he looked at the picture one more time. Why would the picture be time stamped two full weeks after the day it had to have been taken? He looked up at the cold gray sky and back at the photo. He read Frank's letter one more time just to be sure, just to confirm the answer. "Frank, you dumb old fool! You sly old fox!" Replacing the photo back in his shirt, he turned and hurried straight back to the cabin.

Once inside he called, "Shirley? Where are you?"

"I'm in the bedroom, checking the email," came the answer.

"Well, move over, I need the computer...right now!" Almost pushing Shirley aside, Lester slid into the chair in front of the computer keyboard and grabbed the mouse from her hand.

"What is it that couldn't have waited five minutes?"

"Where's the flash drive? Have you had it?"

"It's right there in the drawer where you keep it."

He rummaged through the drawer, casting its contents aside until he located the small black storage device. Inserting the flash drive into the USB slot on the front of the computer, Lester clicked the mouse to open its contents. "Come on, open up!" The flash drive icon morphed into the file directory, listing the contents in alphabetical order. Clicking on a folder labeled 'Gloria's pictures,' he again waited impatiently for the old PC to perform. He pulled the letter from his shirt pocket and glanced at the photo again. Once the file opened, Lester clicked through pictures until finally uttering, "Well, I'll be damned!"

"What is it, Lester?"

Ignoring her, he returned the letter and photo to his pocket, pulled out his phone and dialed the Sheriff's Office. "Hello, this is Lester Pierce. I have some information about a crime. Yes, I'll hold."

"Somebody's at the door," Shirley announced.

Laying the phone down, Lester said, "I'll get it! You let me know when they answer," he said as he left the bedroom. He was surprised to see a very disturbed Dalton Moore and even more surprised that Dalton insisted on coming in.

"Come on in, Dalton. Have a seat. I'm kind of in the middle of something important. Shirley, its Dalton." The ranger pulled a chair out from the table and settled into it uneasily. When Dalton's hand came to rest on his holstered side arm Lester became less concerned about returning to his phone call. "What is it, Dalton? Are you all right?"

"He lied. The son of a bitch was lying from the beginning. And I killed him. I killed the poor kid," Dalton began.

"You killed who? Who lied?"

"I didn't know. I didn't know. But I killed him."

"Shirley!" Lester insisted, "Killed who, Dalton?"

Emerging from the bedroom, Shirley interjected, "Dalton Moore, we've known you for 25 years. Why are you sitting here in our living room blithering on about killing someone? Pull yourself together for God's sake. And take your hand off that gun, you're making us nervous. Why don't you have one of the brownies I just made and relax?"

Taking a deep breath, Dalton shook his head slowly and rambled further. "All I wanted was to put together a little nest egg so I could retire. None of this was supposed to happen."

Looking at Shirley, Lester realized she was just as hard pressed to make sense of the ranger's ramblings. "Come on Dalton, I know you wouldn't kill anybody. Start from the beginning. What are you talking about?"

"He said he'd help me out, but he was just using me, just like he used you and everybody else."

"Who?" Lester asked again. He would have pressed further had it not been for Shirley's wide-eyed look as she glanced out the window. Lester turned to see two sheriffs' cruisers pulling up quietly on the road in front of their cabin. As Dalton continued, Lester watched Sheriff Gardner approach the back door as two deputies made their way around to the front of the cabin.

As if hearing Lester for the first time, Dalton answered matter-of-factly, "Wickham."

A deputy knocked loudly at the front door and announced, "Sheriff's Department!"

Dalton rose from his chair quickly, his hand on his side arm saying only, "Get rid of him!"

As he backed away from the open patio door, sheriff Gardner stepped into the kitchen from the back door, gripped Dalton's left arm firmly from behind and put an iron grasp on Dalton's still holstered gun. "I'll take this while we talk. Come on in." An ashen hue came over Dalton's face as he slumped into his chair again.

"Now, Dalton, what the Hell is going on"?

"I killed Brock Sanford! I didn't mean to, but I'm the reason he's dead!"

"Oh, and how did you do that?" Sheriff Gardner inquired.

"The day he disappeared, I was making rounds of the lake like I always do. When I came to Wickham's place, he flagged me down. He was on that big ZTR mower. He left it running and came over to the truck. He said he needed my help. He said he wanted me to hook on to his boat trailer and back it up so he could mow under it."

"Were you in the habit of doing favors for Wickham?"

"Well, as a matter of fact, I was."

"So how did you come to kill Brock?"

"After we hooked the trailer to my hitch, Wickham went back behind and directed me as I backed. I didn't think much of it at the time, but he stood right on top of that manhole cover, even as he motioned for me to back up right next to his feet. When he stopped me, one of the tandem wheels of that huge trailer was right on top of the lid. I didn't think about it again until Brock's body surfaced and you figured out that he'd been down in that storm sewer. The poor bastard was probably screaming his head off and I couldn't hear him because of Wickham's mower! I didn't mean to, but I'm the one who blocked his only way out. I killed him!"

The Sheriff's apparent relief at hearing Dalton's story only confused Lester further. He thought he even saw a slight smile come to Sheriff Gardner's lips.

"Well, first of all, as you said, you had no way of knowing that Brock was even down there. If anyone is to blame it would be Wickham, since he directed you to park the trailer on the manhole cover. But that's not even my primary concern right now. Actually, I'd like to hear more about why you were so willing to do favors for Wickham."

A very contrite Dalton Moore took a deep breath and looked up at Lester as if he was about to confess to killing JFK. "Lester, I'm sorry I got you involved in this. I never thought any of it would go this far."

"I have no idea what you're talking about. Just spit it out Dalton!"

"Two winters back, I caught Wickham and some of his buddies after they shot a deer and none of them had a license. I was going to ticket them but Wickham took me aside and said if I let it go, he would more than make it up to me. He said he would cut me in on a business deal that would more than finance my retirement. At the time, I didn't see any way to retire on what I had saved or on my state pension, so I just tore up the ticket and gave them a warning. By the time I reconsidered what I had done, Wickham was saying if I changed my mind, he and his buddies would swear to the DNR that I had done this several times before and that they had paid me off. If it came to light that I had let them off I could lose my job, and if they managed to make the DNR chiefs believe their story I'd probably lose my pension. So, from then on, I wasn't willing to cross him."

Dalton directed his gaze down at the carpet of the Pierce's living room and took a deep breath. "Later that winter, Wickham approached me about what he called a business deal. He said he was going to build a supper club and bar out here on the shores of Legion Lake. He knew I wanted to retire in a few years and he asked me if I'd like to manage it. I told him I had no interest in schlepping drinks to boaters after spending 25 years arresting people for drunken boating. He said he understood and dropped it, or at least I thought he did. He came back about two weeks later and told me he had another job in mind for me. He said he'd dropped his plans for the supper club and was instead thinking about investing in agriculture, specifically a hog operation just a few miles up the road from the lake."

"And he wanted you to manage *that* after you retired?"

"Well that's what I thought and I told him he was out of his mind. I not only told him I wanted nothing to do with it because of what it would do to the environment, I said I'd fight him every step of the way."

"So what'd he say to that?"

"The smug son of a bitch just laughed. He said he already had a manager picked out. He said he knew I'd feel that way and that he had just wanted me to know there weren't any hard feelings about the supper club thing."

"So, that's why you were so quick to help him out later?"

"I had no choice. He had me over a barrel."

Looking up at Lester, he explained further. "He knew from the git-go, that you, of all people out here, would fight the CAFO and stir up a negative backlash to it. And, you played right into his plans. Starting with that manure spreader full of pig shit. You see, that's just what he wanted. He never intended to build a CAFO, he just wanted to use the threat of the CAFO to convince the right property owners to sell out to him."

"That son of a bitch!" Lester swore moving toward Dalton, "he played me, all of us, for suckers!"

He was stopped by Shirley who grabbed his hand and pulled him back to her side, saying, "But nobody else would have stepped up to lead the fight to protect the lake and our property. It makes me proud to hear that he thought you were the person who would do just that!"

Sheriff Gardner interrupted, "I was on my way out here to return some of Brock's personal effects to Ashley when my dispatcher patched through Lester's call to me. And, by the way Lester, where is your cell phone?"

"I left it in the bedroom," Lester explained rising to go retrieve it.

"I have it!" explained Shirley. Her proud look turned to embarrassment when she realized it was still connected to the dispatcher. "I put it in my apron pocket when I heard Dalton at the door."

"Well, as I was about to say, I received the coroner's report on Brock Sanford. The coroner determined that Brock died of asphyxiation. He thinks Brock was overcome by sewer gas, which is interesting on its own as there never should have been any sanitary sewage in a storm sewer, unless someone illegally tapped in to the storm sewer with their septic line.

"Somebody like Lee Wickham!"

"What time of day did you back the trailer for Wickham?"

"Right after lunch on the 5th. I know, because I had just come back from town after having my truck serviced."

"The coroner estimates that Brock would have been overcome within minutes of when he entered the storm sewer and everything we know tells us he went in around 9:30 the morning of the 5th. He would have been dead for more than three hours before Wickham stopped you to move the trailer."

"Wait. So, you mean I didn't kill Brock?"

"There's no way you could have."

"So, you're charging Wickham with murder?" insisted Lester.

"That would be pretty hard to prove. He admitted to putting the cover back on the manhole without checking to see if anyone was down in the storm sewer, even though he had seen Brock enter it earlier in the day. We may be looking at a charge of depraved indifference. I still need to go over the evidence we have so far with the County Attorney. And I haven't gotten to the bottom of this sewer gas business either. Actually, we've only scratched the surface. Once we were able to convince Wickham that Brock was actually in the storm drain when he closed the lid, he folded like a road map and spilled the details of his own plan. In an attempt to buy his way out of a charge we actually couldn't have proven, he managed to confess to several lesser charges we *can* prove...with his confession. And if I find out he had a hand in connecting the septic line from his house into the storm sewer he'll be looking at involuntary manslaughter."

"But why was Brock's body so badly beaten up?"

"We'll never know for sure, but it's likely that happened when the heavy rain washed his body out through the storm sewer tile and the flap gate. We have no reason to believe Wickham had anything to do with that."

"So, what happens to Wickham?"

"A jury will have to sort it all out, but I would imagine at the very least his legal expenses will prevent him from building a CAFO *or* a restaurant. Probably already forced him to sell that huge house of his."

"So I *didn't* kill Brock?" Dalton asked as the enormity of what Sheriff Gardner had revealed sunk in.

"At most, you helped Wickham conceal the fact that a man he had already killed was down inside the storm sewer and you had no way of knowing that."

Dalton sat silently, enjoying the relief the sheriff's explanation brought him. But his relief was short-lived. "What about my job? My pension?"

"What about them? I'm pretty sure the law allows you to use your judgment in deciding whether to ticket poachers. Your judgment in this case may well have been poor, but as far as I'm concerned no crime was committed."

"So if Wickham had had a proper septic system installed, he'd probably be in the clear and well on his way to opening a restaurant, but instead he's broke and facing felony charges."

"Yes, and Brock Sanford would likely still be alive."

Chapter 34

With the details of Brock's death known, Lester and Shirley both felt a sense of relief as the sheriff emerged from Ashley's cabin and exited the park via Shoreline Drive. They stood at the deck door entwined in an embrace, watching an inbound flock of geese land clumsily on Legion Lake. "Looks like the lake I remember before all this ugliness came up," Lester observed.

"Let's hope so," she answered. They stood quietly, contemplating all that had been revealed in the past hour. "But what was on the flash drive that was so important?" Shirley asked, breaking the silence.

Lester retrieved the letter and photo from his shirt pocket and handed it to Shirley. After reading the letter and inspecting the photo, Shirley stated simply, "I don't get it?"

"Frank mailed that letter on April 15th. Look at the date on the picture. Its two weeks *after* he mailed it. The date thing on Gloria's camera must have been set two weeks ahead of the actual date. I can't prove it, but I think Frank messed it up when he set up Gloria's camera, and he must surely have realized that once I started to connect Wickham to Brock's disappearance through Gloria's sailboat pictures. But I think he kept it to himself because he wanted to help me prove that Wickham was behind it."

"That's why I was calling the sheriff in the first place. I thought he'd want to know about the inaccuracy in the time line."

"So are you ever going to tell the sheriff?" Shirley asked as she handed the letter and photo back to Lester.

Placing them back into his shirt pocket, Lester considered her question thoughtfully, but before he could answer, he was interrupted by the ringing of Shirley's phone.

"This is Shirley," she answered, "It's Ashley," she explained, covering the phone with her hand. "Sure, we'd love to see you. Come on over. We'll see you soon. Bye." Closing her phone, she explained, "She's coming over to talk."

Within minutes a smiling Ashley Edwards appeared at the patio door toting a car seat insert covered with a small handmade quilt. "Come on in. I'll put on some coffee, or maybe you could join us for lunch?

"No don't bother, I can't stay long."

"And who do we have here?"

"This is little Brock. Brock Lester, to be exact."

A very startled but proud Lester looked at her, tears welling in his eyes. "Oh, you don't want to do that to him. Give him a name he can be proud of."

"Don't worry Lester, when he's old enough to understand what happened to his Dad and what all you did for us, he'll be proud! Very proud!"

Lester could only nod in agreement as he wiped his eyes with his handkerchief.

"Oh, he's absolutely darling. When was he born?"

"February 14th! Is that perfect or what?"

"Can I hold him?"

"Michelle, my friend from work is coming any minute to give me a ride. It takes so long to get him strapped back in I'd better not, but you can as soon as I get home from work."

"You have a job! Where?"

"Brock's old boss, Mr. Groves, gave me a job in his office at the wind power company. Bookkeeping was my best subject in school and he says after I've worked for the company for six months, they'll pay my tuition to a junior college. And, last winter, just when I was so broke, I got a check from Brock's life insurance through the DNR. It was a real lifesaver for us; I didn't even know he had one or that he...thought enough of me to leave it to me," Ashley explained, her voice breaking.

"Nonsense," Shirley scolded as she drew Ashley close for a hug. "I know you meant the world to him. And he'd be very proud of you. And so proud of little Brock."

The honking of a car horn next door interrupted their moment. "Thanks, Shirley! And, you too, Lester. Thank you both so much!"

Covering the car seat insert with the quilt again, she explained, "That's my ride. I gotta go. Can't wait until I have saved enough for a decent car of my own. For little Brock and me."

"Come back after work so we can get to know little Brock. And we can talk."

"Well, I won't be home until after supper. I have another appointment with the attorney...about Brock's estate and Wickham and...well it's real complicated."

"Well, you come over when you can. We'll be here."

"I will, I have so much to tell you. Bye."

Shirley and Lester, having resumed their position at the door, waved goodbye to Ashley and Brock Lester. They stood silently enjoying the quiet solitude Legion Lake once again promised.

"The sheriff didn't stay long. I wonder if Ashley even had time to go over the coroner's report."

"I doubt she wanted to. I know I wouldn't. If I was her, I'd put it away in a safe place until little Brock asks, if he ever does." She gave Lester a sad little smile and squeezed his hand. "Well, I'd better scare up something for lunch," she realized.

"And that lawn isn't going to rake itself either," Lester groaned as he zipped his jacket and stepped out the door. Though neither voiced it, both of them thought things at the lake were definitely getting back to normal.

And in the distance, somewhere just off the shore of Legion Lake, a huge walleye swam away contentedly.

Acknowledgments

Legion Lake, my second book, is yet another piece of work for which I am indebted to my wife, Joan. This book is an expansion of a short story I penned some years ago, titled *One Last Trip*. As my constant sounding board, Joan was the first to lay eyes upon it and reasoned with me that it begged to be expanded into a full-length novel. Thank you, Joan, for believing in me and supporting my writing efforts.

Although I might never have written *Legion Lake* had it not been for my wife's insistence, the final product surely would never have come into existence if not for the editorial efforts of my daughter, Lindsey Kerr. Her hours of proofing and her numerous suggestions about wording and style resulted in a far better book than I could have produced by myself. Perhaps, with her continued assistance, I may someday find the proper words to express my gratitude. Until then, I will continue repayment by working alongside Lindsey to complete her ongoing home improvement projects.

Ruthie's Famous Cinnamon Rolls

3 cups scalded milk
1 cup lard
(add water for a total of 6 cups of liquid)

4 pkgs. Dry yeast
1 cup warm water
1 tsp. sugar

1 tsp. white Karo syrup (no more)
1 cup boiling water
5 lbs. flour
½ cup sugar
2 T. salt
4 cups brown sugar for the pans

Melt lard in milk adding enough water to make a total of 6 cups liquid. Dissolve yeast in warm water and sugar. Let dissolve and bubble up. Mix with dry ingredients (except the brown sugar), knead well until not sticky. Let rise 3 times, punching down twice. Roll ½ inch thick. Spread with soft oleo. Sprinkle with cinnamon and sugar to taste. Roll up and cut into 1 inch slices. Prepare 4, 9 X 13 inch well buttered pans, with 1 cup of brown sugar spread over the bottom of each pan. Put 12 slices into each pan and then turn each one over to get brown sugar on both ends. These will spread out some but not rise. Let rise an hour in pan. Mix Karo syrup and boiling water. Put 1 teaspoon of this over each roll. Bake at 375⁰ for 20 to 30 minutes depending on your oven, until they appear done.

Made in the USA
Middletown, DE
30 March 2019